Eve had risked her life to ensure he got out first.

Why would she put his life before hers? Was it possible she did have feelings for him?

He scrubbed a hand over his face. He was borrowing trouble. When this was over, she would be gone.

Just like before.

There were no words to accurately explain how he'd felt that day in the chapel when she hadn't shown. His whole world had felt as if it were ending. Then he'd diverted all that pain into anger and the need to find the truth.

Had he found it?

He still didn't even know her name. Just Eve. And yet he knew more about her after the past seventy-two hours than he had in two months…before.

Dear Reader,

Thank you so much for choosing my book. This story represents a major milestone for me. *The Bride's Secrets* is the thirty-third COLBY AGENCY story. I am so proud to be a part of the Harlequin Intrigue family. I hope you will enjoy this month's COLBY AGENCY installment, as well as the final book in the trilogy, coming in September.

This year marks a couple more very important milestones as well. For one, this is Harlequin Intrigue's 25th anniversary. Imagine, for twenty-five years Harlequin Intrigue has been bringing readers a breath-stealing ride with suspense, thrills and, of course, romance. Readers never have to wonder what they'll get when they pick up an Intrigue. From the high-octane action, the gut-wrenching suspense, the most wicked villain to the sweet and sizzling connection between the hero and heroine, Intrigue always delivers as promised. Harlequin Intrigue is a fast and furious read each and every month!

Also, this year is Harlequin's 60th anniversary! No other publisher has consistently brought romance to readers in every possible setting and with every imaginable scenario the way Harlequin has. Whether a small-town girl racing toward her future with an international tycoon or a sexy billionairess seeking refuge in the arms of a big strong cowboy far away from her metropolitan home, Harlequin has it covered. Every book, every month features a new and interesting twist on the tried and true as well as in cutting edge, previously uncharted territory. Escape, that's what Harlequin has given readers for more than half a century.

So, turn the page and escape with me!

Best,

Debra Webb

DEBRA WEBB

THE BRIDE'S SECRETS

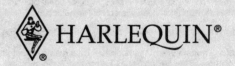

HARLEQUIN®

TORONTO • NEW YORK • LONDON
AMSTERDAM • PARIS • SYDNEY • HAMBURG
STOCKHOLM • ATHENS • TOKYO • MILAN • MADRID
PRAGUE • WARSAW • BUDAPEST • AUCKLAND

Recycling programs for this product may not exist in your area.

ISBN-13: 978-0-373-69418-1

THE BRIDE'S SECRETS

Copyright © 2009 by Debra Webb

www.eHarlequin.com

Printed in U.S.A.

ABOUT THE AUTHOR

Debra Webb was born in Scottsboro, Alabama, to parents who taught her that anything is possible if you want it bad enough. She began writing at age nine. Eventually, she met and married the man of her dreams, and tried some other occupations, including selling vacuum cleaners, working in a factory, a daycare center, a hospital and a department store. When her husband joined the military, they moved to Berlin, Germany, and Debra became a secretary in the commanding general's office. By 1985 they were back in the States, and finally moved to Tennessee, to a small town where everyone knows everyone else. With the support of her husband and two beautiful daughters, Debra took up writing again, looking to mysteries and movies for inspiration. In 1998, her dream of writing for Harlequin Books came true. You can write to Debra with your comments at P.O. Box 64, Huntland, Tennessee 37345, or visit her Web site at www.debrawebb.com to find out exciting news about her next book.

Books by Debra Webb

HARLEQUIN INTRIGUE
891—PERSON OF INTEREST
909—INVESTIGATING 101*
916—RAW TALENT*
934—THE HIDDEN HEIR*
951—A COLBY CHRISTMAS*
983—A SOLDIER'S OATH†
989—HOSTAGE SITUATION†
995—COLBY VS. COLBY†
1023—COLBY REBUILT*
1042—GUARDIAN ANGEL*
1071—IDENTITY UNKNOWN*
1092—MOTIVE: SECRET BABY
1108—SECRETS IN FOUR CORNERS
1145—SMALL-TOWN SECRETS††
1151—THE BRIDE'S SECRETS††

*Colby Agency
†The Equalizers
††Colby Agency: Elite Reconnaissance Division

CAST OF CHARACTERS

J. T. Baxley—Colby Agency investigator. He was left at the altar by his bride a mere two weeks ago. He wants to know why.

Eve Mattson—She isn't who she seems to be. Can J.T. trust anything she says?

Terrence Arenas—J.T.'s former colleague. Arenas is an insurance fraud investigator.

Leonard Jamison—He is certain the insurance company cheated his wife, and now his wife is dead.

Damon Howe—He worked closest with Arenas at the insurance company. Is he hiding the truth?

Rebecca James—She is J.T.'s only connection to his old life at the insurance company. Can she help him find the truth?

Victoria Colby-Camp—The head of the Colby Agency.

Jamie Colby—Victoria's granddaughter.

Merrilee Walters—The newest member of the Colby Agency.

Errol Leberman—An evil that has haunted the Colby name for decades.

Chapter One

Chicago, 9:30 a.m.

The Colby Agency's conference room overflowed with staff members. All were present for this morning's meeting, except the newest investigator on staff. Well, the newest member until their recent hire of Merrilee Walters. J. T. Baxley had taken a bullet last night while serving on Victoria's personal security detail.

Victoria Colby-Camp sat at the head of the long Mahogany table, listening as Ian Michaels reviewed the tightened security measures. Last night's attack had confirmed the worst.

The risk to her granddaughter's safety was no longer mere theory or rumor. It was real.

Too real.

Increasing fear pumped through Victoria's veins with every frantic beat of her heart. Nothing she or her people had done so far had given them the answers for which they searched.

Every lead turned into a dead end.

Yet, someone out there continued to attempt to get to her granddaughter.

Her loyal staff began filing out of the room. Victoria blinked, dragged her focus back to the present. She hadn't realized Ian had concluded his briefing.

Ian settled in a chair to her right; Simon Ruhl did the same on her left.

These two men were Victoria's most trusted associates, professional and personal. Yet, like her, they could only react to the threat. Whoever was behind this had burrowed so deeply beneath multiple ambiguous layers of disinformation that it would take time—precious time—to ferret them out.

This was the first occasion in the Colby Agency's prestigious history that Victoria had no choice but to admit they were mystified.

"Last night—" Simon kicked off the overview of the few known facts "—an attempt was made to abduct Jamie."

The sound of a bullet shattering the windshield, killing the driver, echoed through Victoria's mind. Three were dead, including two unidentified males involved in the abduction attempt. Two others had fled the scene. Though J. T. Baxley had taken a bullet; he'd been treated and released at the E.R. Still, the risk to his life—to her granddaughter's—had shaken Victoria to the core.

"Have we learned anything new?" Otherwise she saw no need to go over those horrendous details yet again. Another image, this one of her pulling the trigger, ending the life of the man with the gun aimed at her face, erupted in her mind.

She'd had no choice…. And still, the realization deeply disturbed her.

Rather than answering her question, Ian and Simon exchanged a long look. Now she understood.

"You believe it's an inside job." It pained Victoria to say the words.

"Yes," Ian confirmed.

"That's the only way anyone could have known your schedule for last evening," Simon clarified. "None of us want to believe that's possible."

"At this point—" Ian picked up where Simon left off "—we have to face that undeniable possibility."

Victoria took a breath, her chest tightening with the emotions charging through her. "Do you have a suspect?"

Her closest confidants shared another look.

She wasn't going to like their conclusion. Victoria wasn't happy with the concept in general, but obviously the answer was going to be even less palatable.

"J. T. Baxley," Ian stated.

J.T.? "I was at his christening." Victoria had just graduated from university at the time. One of her dearest friends had opted for marriage over college, and J.T. had been her first and only child.

Simon nodded his understanding. "We fully understand that you've known J.T. and his family for years. But he was one of the few who had access to last night's schedule."

That was true. J.T. had been a part of her security detail last night. And he'd paid the price.

Victoria shook her head. "This simply isn't possible." She had sought out J.T. when his mother had relayed that he had left the insurance industry. Victoria had hoped for years that she would be able to lure him to the Colby Agency. Only a few months ago that opportunity had arisen. He'd signed on as a member of her Reconnaissance group.

"J.T. ignored the all-hands call this morning."

Simon's announcement sent a new kind of fear throttling through Victoria. "Has anyone checked on him?" The man had been shot for God's sake. Though the shot appeared to have been clean, in and out of the biceps with no apparent serious damage, there was always the chance something had been missed. With any sort of penetrating wound, internal bleeding was always a concern. She'd thought nothing of his absence, considering what he'd gone through last night.

"I went to his home myself," Ian assured her. "He wasn't there, but the door was unlocked. There was no indication he'd slept in his bed. Nothing appeared to be missing. His cell phone was on the kitchen counter, and his car was in the garage."

"Then we should be concerned for his safety," Victoria argued, "not suspicious of his participation in this deception." The suggestion was preposterous. J.T. was as trustworthy and reliable as the passing of time.

"J.T. may not have been a willing participant," Simon qualified. "We've learned some unsettling details regarding his former fiancée."

A frown worried Victoria's brow. J.T. had been devastated when his bride-to-be hadn't shown. He'd literally been left at the altar. That had been a mere two weeks ago. Rather than having him take on another agency assignment Victoria had allowed him to focus on trying to find out what had happened to the woman, who seemed to have simply vanished. The agony of watching his desperation play out tortured her even now as she considered his plight.

"Explain," Victoria prompted her closest confidants.

"We don't have in-depth details as of yet," Ian offered. "But we have uncovered a number of aliases she has operated under during the past six or seven years. From all appearances, Eve Mattson is a serious scam artist. She may have been playing J.T. as a part of setting the stage for Jamie's abduction."

Victoria looked from Ian to Simon. "Find J.T. Whoever this Eve Mattson is or was, we owe it to J.T. to give him the benefit of the doubt. If he's in trouble, we'll back him up."

Victoria would not let J.T. down. If he had somehow been drawn into this plan against Victoria's granddaughter, it would have been unknowingly and certainly unwilling.

"Also, find out who Eve Mattson is," Victoria went on. "I promised J.T. I wouldn't interfere with his search for his missing bride-to-be, but this news changes everything. If Eve Mattson is involved in the plan to harm my granddaughter, I want her found and the truth extracted." Fury detonated inside Victoria. "Whoever is behind this is going to rue the day they picked the Colby Agency as a target."

If it was the last thing Victoria did, all involved would pay the fiddler a hefty price for this dance.

Chapter Two

J.T. groaned. He heard the sound…wanted to open his eyes, to wake up, but his throbbing brain just wouldn't make the necessary transition.

Wake up!

He needed to wake up. Something was very wrong.

His eyelids cracked open, but bright light slammed them shut once more.

Wake up, damn it!

With tremendous effort his eyelids split open again.

Where was he?

His booted feet rested on a stone or concrete floor. Nylon twine tethered his ankles to what looked like chair legs.

Raise your head.

Slowly, his head moved. Pain shattered his skull. He groaned.

Damn.

What the hell had happened to him?

His eyes opened a little wider. Stark gray walls. He tried to reach up and touch his head. The throbbing above his right ear roared. His fingers fisted in reaction to the pain. He twisted his wrists, couldn't move his hands.

He blinked, focused his gaze on his hands…his arms.

His wrists were secured to the chair's arms with that same orange nylon twine.

Okay. *Think!* He was manacled to a chair. In an empty room. He forced his head to move ever so slightly, ever so slowly from side to side. Yep. No furnishings.

Where was the light coming from?

He moved his head back, peered through squinted eyes at the ceiling. A single bare bulb glared at him from a high ceiling.

Basement?

Garage?

How had he gotten here?

J.T. closed his eyes and summoned the last details he recalled.

He'd been working Victoria's security detail. There had been a shootout with four unidentified gunmen. One had escaped, two were killed. Three counting Victoria's driver.

J.T. had been shot.

Instinctively he tried to lift his right hand to inspect his left arm. Couldn't. Clean shot through the left biceps.

As if the memory had prompted the pain, an ache speared through his biceps.

After J.T. was treated at the E.R., Ian had driven him home. He'd waved as Ian drove away, walked onto his porch, and unlocked the door. J.T. remembered going inside and then…

Pain detonated in his skull once more.

Someone had attacked him.

Fury bolted through him. He jerked at his bindings. Gritted his teeth against the pain.

If this had something to do with Victoria or her granddaughter, his captor should just go ahead and kill him. No way was he giving away any information, much less participating in whatever the scheme might be.

Sweat streamed down his face as he struggled to free himself.

He twisted, squirmed, pulled.

Eventually the fatigue and pain forced him to surrender the battle.

He wasn't going anywhere.

The slide of metal against metal brought his head up.

Setting his jaw hard against the pain, he used his

body weight and his waning strength to shake and jerk the chair to the right. The door was at his back. He needed to turn around so that he could see the enemy coming. A little farther. *Move,* he commanded.

Harder and harder he jerked and twisted. The chair scooted and swayed precariously.

As the door opened, he managed a final jerk, hauling himself and the chair to face that direction.

A form appeared in the doorway. He blinked. Told himself to look again.

It couldn't be.

"I see you're still alive."

Impossible.

Fury exploded in his veins. "Eve." The name left a bitter taste on his tongue.

She closed the door behind her and leaned against it. "I thought you'd be happy to see me."

"I don't know what the hell you think you're doing," he growled even as the agony screamed in his skull. A shudder rocked through him. "But if you want to survive this, you'd better cut me loose."

She cocked her head. "Hmm…I don't think so."

"Who put you up to this?" The demand echoed in the deserted room.

"No one." She pushed away from the door and started toward him, one slow, measured step at a time. "This was entirely my idea."

Every single muscle in his body tensed as she neared. She walked all the way around him. His nostrils flared wide in an effort to draw in her scent. He cursed his body for its betrayal.

Yes, he was glad to see that she was alive and apparently well.

But, by God, he wanted some answers and he wanted them now!

"Whatever they're paying you," he informed her, "Victoria Colby-Camp will see that you understand it wasn't nearly enough."

Eve laughed softly, the sound aching through him. How had he fallen so madly in love with a woman he hadn't even known?

"I'm not afraid of your employer, J.T." She leaned close, close enough that he could feel her breath on his ear. "I'm not afraid of anyone. Never have been." She straightened away from him. "So don't waste your breath threatening me. It won't work, and it's a waste of energy you'll need later."

Her slow circling continued until she stood before him, face-to-face.

"Who are you?" The harshly uttered words were fraught with emotion he couldn't restrain. Damn her. She'd fooled him…betrayed him on every level. The idea made him sick to his stomach.

She put her hands on her hips and seemed to mull

over his question a long moment. Then her startlingly blue gaze settled on his once more. "Even I'm not sure about the answer to that one anymore." She stepped closer. "But I know who you are." She leaned forward. "And I also know that you're a marked man, Mr. Baxley. Either you do as I tell you or you die. Seems like an easy choice to me."

He stared into those dazzling eyes, his gut clenching with opposing emotions. "How can you be a part of this? Jamie Colby is just a child." That he could have been fooled so completely worsened the misery in his gut.

The woman he had known as Eve Mattson, braced her hands on his arms and put her face in his. "What you think of me is irrelevant. My mission is all that matters."

"Are they doing this for the money?" His fingers curled into fists even as his skin beneath where her palms rested tingled with desire from her touch. He silently cursed himself. Hated that he could still want her so desperately.

She didn't answer immediately. Instead, she studied his face, searched his eyes. A fleeting flicker of some emotion he couldn't quite label, regret perhaps, passed across her face—the face he'd cherished with all his heart. The same one that had haunted his dreams every night since she had disappeared.

"I can tell you one thing for certain," she said, her voice achingly soft and familiar. "It's definitely about money."

He held her eyes. Wished he could understand how the woman with whom he'd made love…had planned to spend the rest of his life…could be so cold. Where was the heart he'd been sure he'd touched?

She jerked away from him as if his thoughts had reached out, speared her in that chest that apparently harbored only emptiness.

Then she turned and started for the door.

"Don't do this," he urged, the plea all too real on far too many levels.

She stopped and turned back to him. "If it makes you feel any better, this has nothing to do with the Colby agency or the kid."

What the hell? On cue, his injured arm burned where the bullet had passed through his flesh. "I don't believe you. If this isn't about the Colby Agency, then what's it about?"

"You, J.T." She reached for the door, looking back over her shoulder at him. "It's about you."

Chapter Three

10:30 p.m.

Eve scanned the shoreline, then the street.

No sign of trouble yet.

She lowered the binoculars. It wouldn't last. And she needed more time. Getting J.T. out of his house and into her car hadn't been easy. He'd been out cold. But not as cold as the scumbag who'd been waiting for him to come home. She'd taken care of that situation without breaking a sweat. Dumping his body in the water once they'd gotten here had been an easy cleanup. The real work had been moving J.T. to this location before he regained consciousness. She'd been forced to take an extra step to ensure he didn't rouse too soon.

Now he was wide awake.

And they were close.

Whoever the hell *they* were.

A breath hissed from her lips as she tucked the binoculars into her shoulder bag. She'd been in this business a long time. Every job she accepted came with certain risks. It wasn't rocket science. Just work. Get in, get the goods, whatever the goods happened to be, and get out.

She was very good at her job. Damned good. Whatever persona was required, she could pull it off. She researched the required occupation to the point that she appeared every bit the experienced expert. Not once in nearly a decade had her skills been questioned.

For her, creating a new identity and pulling it off was—in a word—simple.

But not this time.

But then, she'd never played the part of fiancée. Lover, yes. Mistress, of course. But never this *intimate* character.

Her fingers clenched.

Just a job. That was all this had been. She had to keep that fact in mind. The only reason she was still hanging around the Windy City was because no one—no one—double-crossed her.

Until she neutralized this situation, she wasn't going anywhere.

He wasn't going to make it easy.

Anticipation zipped along her nerve endings. The need to draw his scent into her lungs…to touch his skin was a palpable force inside her. No one had ever gotten that far beneath her carefully constructed exterior. She steeled herself to block the reaction. Again she reminded herself that he was part of the job, nothing more. And the job wasn't finished yet.

Not until she got the bastard who'd double-crossed her.

And ensured that J.T. didn't pay the price.

If this guy thought J.T. was his biggest problem, he had no idea what he'd done. Crossing her had been a serious mistake.

Now she was his biggest problem.

He would soon understand just how big that problem was going to be.

As if the thought had summoned his minions, movement below snagged her attention. She watched from the fourth-floor window as four—no, five—men moved toward the warehouse.

"It's showtime." She turned away from the window and headed for the stairs. If she'd been smart, she would have moved already.

Things didn't always go as planned. That was why her motto remained firm. *Always have a backup plan.* And an exit strategy for every occasion.

Timing was where she'd fallen down tonight.

She jogged down the three flights of stairs to her destination and burst through the door.

"We have to move. Now."

Fists clenched, J.T. glared at her. "Whatever you're involved in, I'm not a part of it." He moved his head from side to side. "The *we* that included you and I ended the day you didn't show up for our wedding."

Not exactly original, but the statement had been one he'd likely wanted to say to her for two weeks now. He'd gotten that out of the way. Good for him.

She hated to do it this way, but…what the hell. Her right hand rammed into her bag, and her fingers closed around the butt of her Glock. "Save it, J.T." She drew the weapon. "We don't have time."

Dropping into a crouch, she retrieved the knife from her bag with her free hand and cut the bindings from around his ankles with one quick swipe to each. She stood and looked him dead in the eyes. "Give me any trouble and we'll both be dead in—" she hummed a note "—about three minutes."

"You carry a weapon?"

The question hit its mark. Maybe not the question, but the way he'd asked it. He'd believed in her. Swallowed her profile hook, line and sinker. She flinched.

She never flinched. But somehow it bothered her that he was disappointed. In *her.*

"Trust me," she warned. "We don't have time for this."

He stared her dead in the eyes.

"Give me one good reason I should trust you for a second."

That he no longer trusted her…hurt. And it shouldn't have.

"Because you want to stay alive."

A door bursting open echoed in the distance.

The enemy was in the building.

There was no more time to talk.

The decision had to be made now.

"Cut me loose."

His tone left no room for doubt. He didn't trust her. Not one iota. But he wasn't stupid. He would accept her word…for the moment.

Two swipes of the blade and he was free.

She sheathed the knife in her bag and headed for the rear exit, keeping one eye on his every move.

He stood, steadied himself and followed the path she'd taken.

Maybe this wouldn't be so difficult after all.

In the corridor she stayed close to the wall. J.T. did the same. The consuming quiet was disturbing. The enemy was inside. But where?

Part of her wanted to drop back and take at least one of the enemy out of action, but not completely out. She needed information. The scumbag at J.T.'s house had forced her hand. She'd had no choice but to take him out. Couldn't question a dead man.

"This way," she whispered to the man sticking close behind her.

He didn't question her decision, just followed as she took a side corridor that would lead to the outside. She'd spotted five men; taking on five single-handedly wasn't something she wanted to do under the circumstances. J.T. was wounded, not seriously but wounded all the same. Not to mention he wasn't exactly an ally. And she couldn't risk arming him.

At the exit she hesitated, listened.

J.T. gestured to his right and whispered, "Maybe thirty yards behind us."

Had he heard something she hadn't? Then she heard it, too. The whisper of rubber soles on concrete floors. The slightest vibration in the air.

He was good…. But then she'd known that.

She pushed through the exit, uncaring of the metal-on-metal sound the lock mechanism made. No time to care. *Keep moving.*

Down the exterior steps. Quickly. She glanced back once to ensure J.T. was right behind her. He hadn't slowed down or second-guessed the need to escape.

At least so far.

She hit the ground running. The dock was above their heads. They'd scarcely cleared the exterior maintenance area when she heard the exit they'd used reopen.

The iron stairs groaned with the weight of the enemy's descent.

Damn, they were close.

"The water," she said to J.T., knowing he would understand.

Eve rushed toward the bank that wound up to the dock. Her shoes bogged down in the damp earth. She hadn't factored in today's rain.

Her feet slid. She braced her free hand against the ground rising up to greet her and ordered her legs to keep moving.

Scrambling onto the dock, she regained her balance and rushed forward. The warehouse's rear dock jutted out over the water. A single cargo boat floated in the calm waters. A boat would be handy about now but there was no time to attempt getting it started and backed away from the dock.

At any second the enemy would reach their position.

No time to evaluate the situation.

"Jump," she ordered.

She shoved the Glock into her waistband and dropped feetfirst into the water. Instinctively, she held her breath just before the cool depth engulfed her.

A surge of water from her left told her J.T. had obeyed her command.

Something else that wouldn't last.

A rip through the water jerked her attention to her right. She couldn't see anything but she recognized the sound.

Gunfire.

Damn.

She dove deeper. Pushed through the dark depths, headed for the craggy shoreline in the distance. The goal was to get as far from the dock—and the reach of the enemy—as possible before surfacing.

J.T. cut through the water next to her.

She hoped like hell his strength would hold out.

Her lungs burned.

Just move.

She pushed harder.

Bullets sliced through the water.

To her right…too close.

Damn.

She swam harder. Kept her body beneath the murky surface when the urge to rise grew stronger.

Fight the urge to breathe.

Push! Keep going!

One last lunge forward.

She needed air.

Her face broke the surface.

Gasping for oxygen, she swam hard. Stroke after stroke. Harder. *Push!*

Her fingertips brushed the rocks of the shore.

Almost there.

Where the hell was J.T.?

She whipped around.

He'd surfaced, was breathing hard. Not close enough for her comfort.

The dark figures on the dock were still firing. The bullets cut through the surface of the water. The muffled sound told her they were using silencers.

That was to her benefit. Silencers decreased the accuracy of every shot and lessened the range. Still, they weren't in the clear just yet.

She grabbed for the rocks. Scrambled through the darkness. Bumped her knee on a boulder. Cursed. Move! Move!

Burrowing into the waist-deep grass, she crawled forward. Faster. Pushed harder. She needed as much distance as possible.

Shots pinged on the rocks.

She zigzagged to avoid any stray shots that made it this far.

J.T. scrambled alongside her.

He was breathing hard.

They had to stay close to the ground until they reached the next row of warehouses. Even though she was relatively certain they were out of range at this point, she wasn't taking any risks.

And she wasn't slowing down.

J.T. had to keep up.

The splat of a bullet hitting the ground next to her had her rolling left. Maybe they weren't completely out of range.

She bumped J.T. He grunted.

His injured arm. Damn it.

She could apologize later.

Half a dozen more yards.

Almost in the clear.

As she reached the cover of the alley between the first two warehouses, she tensed.

Silence.

She glanced back at the dock.

Deserted.

The enemy was on the move.

Time to run.

Her car was parked another block down.

Pushing to her feet, she sprinted forward. The wet bag dragged at her shoulder. Her soggy shoes weighed down her feet.

She ignored both.

By the time she reached the lot where her car was parked, she had dug the keys from her pocket and clicked the fob.

Seconds later she was behind the wheel.

She hit the ignition as J.T. collapsed into the passenger seat.

Tires squealed as she spun out of the parking slot.

"What the hell did you do to me?"

From the corner of her eye she watched him shake his head in an attempt to clear it.

He wouldn't be happy when she told him about the tranquilizer.

She'd needed him cooperative; otherwise no plan would work. A drug-induced state of unconsciousness had been the fastest and most efficient method to ensure his continued solidarity.

"I can't really talk right now." She weaved into the right lane as the street widened to four lanes. What she needed was traffic. It was Saturday night—shouldn't be that difficult to find as soon as they were out of the old warehouse district.

A glance in the rearview mirror warned that their unwanted company had caught up.

Sensing her tension, J.T. turned to peer over his left shoulder.

"I hope you have a plan B."

She shot him a look. "There's always plan G." Then she pulled the Glock out of her waistband.

Cutting the steering wheel left, she slid between

two vehicles. Veering then to the right, she put several cars between hers and the enemy.

She was betting they wouldn't pull out the firepower in the open like this, but a woman could never be too sure when it came to an unknown enemy.

Deep blending was the way to go.

Two traffic lights ahead the marquis of a movie theater provided exactly the opportunity she was looking for.

The digital numbers of the dashboard's clock indicated it was just past midnight. Perfect timing. The late movie would be purging its audience into the crowd of teenagers who liked hanging out in the parking lot.

Plenty of cover for blending in.

She took a hard right onto the property that sported a twelve-screen theater, numerous fastfood hot spots and a chain superstore. Speeding across the lot, she selected a lane of parking slots. Pulling in as close to the theater entrance as possible, she shut off the engine and reached for her door.

"Let's go."

Thankfully he didn't argue.

Rounding the hood of her car, she shoved the Glock into her bag, then wrapped her arm around J.T.'s and merged into the milling crowd.

With her free hand she finger combed her long hair. It was soaked, as were her clothes. Her shoes squished with every step. The kids she bumped into noticed, gave her the death ray.

They just didn't know.

As she and J.T. moved in closer to the building, she grabbed a baseball cap from an innocent by-stander. The crowd made it easy. The kid who owned the cap had made it even easier by stuffing it bill first into his waistband at the small of his back.

Pushing through the loitering crowd, Eve made her way to the side of the building next to the main entrance, pushed J.T. against the wall and dropped her bag to the ground. She peeled off her T-shirt and let it join her bag on the pavement.

His gaze instantly zeroed in on her breasts, where the camisole she wore had glued to her skin like an extra layer. A zing of desire shot through her veins.

Not the time.

With a flick of her wrist, she twisted her hair up and clamped the cap atop the blond mass.

"They're coming," J.T. muttered as he gazed at some point beyond her.

"Yeah, I know." She planted her palms against the wall on either side of him and leaned in. "Keep your eyes open. Let me know when they're inside."

Then she planted her lips on his.

Chapter Four

Two weeks.

Fourteen days and nights.

J.T. had yearned to feel her lips against his…had ached to touch her…to hold her.

He forgot all about her order. His eyes closed. His arms went around her. The move was pure instinct.

He'd fallen so fast, had loved her so damned much.

But that had been before.

Before she'd stood him up on the most important day of their lives.

His eyes opened.

Fury firmed his resolve.

She tensed, sensing his change.

He clutched her waist. Pushed her a few inches away.

"Who the hell are you?" he muttered, his voice thick with the need throttling through his body.

"Did they go inside?"

He blinked. Her focus was on the now…the situation. He should have known he was the only one affected by the meshing of lips.

Stupid, J.T. Truly stupid.

The idea that bullets had been flying around them as they'd fled that warehouse suddenly bobbed to the surface of all the questions and emotions churning in his confused brain.

He cut his attention to the building's front entrance. Three of the five who'd followed them from the dock pushed their way into the theater's lobby. "Three just went inside."

"One or more will be sticking with my car." She kept her gaze carefully locked on his. "You don't see number five?"

"Wait." His gaze clocked the movements of an older man, one who definitely didn't fit in with the teenage crowd all around them. "He's moving in the opposite direction."

"Excellent."

She grabbed his hand and started cutting through the crowd. He shouldered between the bodies, staying close behind her.

He had questions for her. So damned many questions. Those would have to wait until they were out of immediate danger.

Could she be telling the truth?

Why would these guys be after him?

He'd worked a couple of Colby Agency assignments with two of the other investigators but nothing on his own yet. He'd made no enemies in that short time or on either of those assignments. His former career in insurance had been as a claims investigator. He'd certainly made no enemies there. His work had been straightforward—review the closed files and ensure that the *i*'s were dotted and the *t*'s crossed.

J.T. shook off the situation analysis. Tried to think clearly about the moment.

No matter how he weighed it, he shouldn't be here with Eve. What was he doing following her? Whatever she was into had nothing to do with him. Obviously she'd drugged him. The knock on the head wouldn't have dulled his reactions to this degree.

When he would have stalled to demand more answers, she took a left, headed for a couple of teenagers loading into a minivan.

"Hey."

The kid climbing behind the wheel looked back.

"Can you give us a ride?"

J.T. started to advise Eve not to waste her time. The driver looked ready to bolt. As he well should. Giving rides to strangers was a bad idea.

"I'll give you a hundred bucks," Eve tacked on.

The driver exchanged a look with his passenger, who'd already climbed into the van.

Eve pulled a couple of bills from her shoulder bag. "Two if you hurry."

The driver stared at the cash and licked his lips. "You have to pay me now."

"Are you crazy?" the passenger muttered to his friend.

Eve handed the driver a hundred. "One now." She reached for the van's sliding door. "One when we get to our destination." She opened the door and climbed in before he'd had time to answer.

This was insane, but J.T. climbed in behind her all the same.

"What the hell you doing?" the passenger asked the driver. He was clearly a lot more rational than his friend.

"Just shut up," the driver advised as he backed out of the space.

For J.T.'s eyes only, Eve pointed to the car she'd parked a couple of lanes away. Sure enough, a man loitered next to it.

J.T. couldn't deny the threat had been real. But he was certain this wasn't about him, despite what she had said.

"Where to?"

Eve turned her attention to the driver.

Before she could answer, J.T. gave the kid the address of the closest police precinct. "I'll give you twice what she offered if we go there first."

"You got it, mister."

Eve glared at J.T. "You're going to make this hard, aren't you?"

He cut her a sideways glance. "I don't know what you're up to, and I don't care. But, for me, it's *over.*"

That she winced on the final word shouldn't have reached out and put a chokehold on his throat. But it did.

They were out of the parking lot and a full two blocks down the street before Eve reacted.

She scooted forward. "Don't pay any attention to my friend," she said to the driver. "We're going to the Pier. You'll drop us off there, and I'll give you the other hundred, as agreed."

"No way," the driver argued. "He said he'd give me twice as much."

Eve reached into the bag she kept close to her side and withdrew the Glock. "But I'm the one with the gun," she countered.

The kid's head whipped to the right.

"Watch it, man!" his friend shouted.

Horns blared.

The driver turned the car back over the line he'd crossed.

"The Pier." Eve reminded him. "Straight there." She instructed him on the most direct route. "Make it fast, but stay close to the speed limit."

Eve leaned back in her seat and divided her attention between the driver and J.T., but she kept the Glock aimed directly at him.

She was not happy.

Tough.

Neither was he.

She'd better brace herself. Once they were at their new destination, this reunion was over.

J.T. decided then and there that he no longer cared about the why. He'd spent two weeks tearing himself apart, desperately seeking the truth.

That was the moment the situation crystallized: in a stranger's minivan with the business end of a Glock directed at him.

It didn't matter why. She had dumped him. Disappeared. It was over.

Who she was or what she was into had nothing to do with him, no matter what she said.

He hadn't recognized the five men who'd shot at them, then gave chase. He damned sure didn't recognize the woman sitting a scarce eighteen inches away.

Long, silent minutes later the driver took the final turn to the Pier.

"Drive to the end of the block," Eve instructed, breaking the long stretch of intense quiet. "We'll get out at the intersection."

"Whatever you say, lady."

J.T. steeled for making his break.

His cell phone and wallet were missing. But he wasn't concerned. He would find someone, even at this hour, around the Pier. All he needed was one minute on a cell phone, and help from the Colby Agency would be dispatched.

The van braked to a stop.

Eve shoved the second hundred at the driver. "Thanks, kid." She reached for the sliding door on her side. "And remember, this never happened."

The kid stared at the money in his hand. "That part could be extra." His greedy gaze lit up with hope.

"That's all you get, kid," Eve warned. "Don't push your luck."

"But he said—" the kid started to argue.

"He," Eve interrupted, "doesn't have a weapon."

The kid backed off. "Whatever you say, lady."

J.T. got out on his side of the vehicle. He started in the direction of the Pier. Didn't look back.

The van rolled away from the curb, passing him as it barreled forward.

"You're making a mistake," Eve shouted at his back.

He kept walking, refusing to spare even a backward glance.

She hustled up next to him. "You're going with me, J.T."

He didn't slow his stride. "Not a chance."

She stopped.

He kept walking.

The sound of a car door closing told him she'd gotten into one of the vehicles lining the curb.

Apparently she'd had a plan B. He hadn't recognized the vehicle they'd left at the movie theater. Probably a rental. Who knew? He didn't know her at all. Didn't know what she liked…what she drove… that she had a fetish for guns.

Nothing.

He'd been a fool.

A few seconds later a car slowed on the street next to him. The passenger-side window powered down. "Get in the car, J.T."

He ignored her order.

She braked hard, got out. "We're wasting time," she shouted over the top of the car. "Get in now!"

He hesitated, turned to stare at her. "Or what? You'll shoot." He sent a pointed look at the weapon in her hand.

She didn't immediately answer.

"So shoot." He turned away and started forward again.

"Give me two hours," she called after him. "I'll explain everything."

Something had changed in her voice. There was a desperation there…a fear…almost.

He shook his head, wasn't going to be fooled by her again. Whatever she said, this couldn't have anything to do with him.

And he was out of here.

"J.T., please. I need your help."

His step faltered. He told himself to keep walking, but his feet failed him.

"Just hear me out," she pleaded. "That's all I'm asking."

Fury pulsed in his jaw. He wanted to pretend the past couple of months had never happened. That he hadn't met and fallen in love with her.

The men who'd shot at them…the chase… zoomed into vivid focus in his mind.

She was in trouble. Obviously. Whatever it was about, she needed help. He couldn't deny that singular fact.

Nor could he deny another glaring fact.

He couldn't just walk away and pretend he no longer cared.

He did care.

Damn him.

Mentally kicking himself for being a fool, he changed directions and strode up to the car waiting in the street. The sparse traffic glided around her, the other cars' occupants likely assuming the two were in the midst of a lovers' spat.

He stopped at the passenger door and stared at her across the car's roof. "Two hours," he confirmed. "You have two hours to explain yourself, and then I'm gone."

She nodded, her blue eyes wide with worry. Her blond hair was still damp and clung to her face like tendrils of silk.

He said nothing more. Got into the car.

She settled behind the wheel and put the vehicle in Drive.

"Where are we going?"

She glanced at him before rolling forward. "Where we should have gone two weeks ago."

He frowned. Two weeks ago they would have gone on…

Their honeymoon?

Chapter Five

Crystal Lake, 2:00 a.m.

Eve parked beneath the canopy of trees near the rented cabin. The lack of moonlight left them in darkness, which was just as well, since she was relatively sure she wouldn't like what she saw in J.T.'s brown eyes.

He hadn't said a word since they'd left Chicago. Almost an hour later, her nerves were completely frayed. So many times she'd wanted to kick off the conversation. Just get it over with. But she couldn't take the risk. She'd needed him away from the city, and the danger, before she reopened communication.

This far out he wasn't likely to walk away.

She'd taken his cell phone and wallet. Until she had him convinced of her theory, she needed him basically at her mercy.

Shooting him wasn't an option.

She got out of the car, reached into the backseat and grabbed her bag and stalked to the cabin. The honeymoon arrangements had been her idea. Convincing J.T. to stay close to home after the wedding, owing to her work commitments, had been easy enough. She'd rented the cabin for a month, rather than the weekend she'd told him about. Having a backup plan was her motto. She never left home without one.

Digging the key from her soggy bag, she breathed a sigh of relief for the first time in weeks. Two to be exact.

But this was far from over.

"If this is a joke, I'm not amused."

It wasn't a joke and she wasn't amused, either. This was about survival.

"We can talk inside."

She pushed through the door and left it open. If she was lucky, he would follow without any additional persuasion.

But then—she flipped on a light and turned to wait for his entrance—she'd never been one to wait on luck. Her fingers itched to reach into her bag and grab the Glock, make this easy.

Easy wouldn't work with J.T. He had to come around on his own terms. She'd learned that, if nothing else, in the couple of months they'd spent together.

Tall and gorgeous as ever, he loomed in the doorway, his T-shirt still damp and clinging to his chest. The bloody stain on his left sleeve a reminder that he'd been injured. She didn't know all the details related to last night's attack, but she was certain the incident had nothing to do with *their* situation. He'd mentioned the head of the Colby Agency's grandchild. Maybe the injury had something to do with that.

Before she could stop herself, her gaze had traveled down the length of him. From his dark hair and eyes to the still-soggy trousers molded to his muscled thighs. Her pulse skipped in spite of her determination not to react to him physically. Apparently that wasn't a facet of this situation she had under control just yet.

That was something else she'd learned recently. She wasn't completely immune to certain…*things*.

And he was one of them.

Just when she thought maybe she might need her Glock after all, he stepped into the room and closed the door. Would wonders never cease?

He'd promised her two hours. The clock was ticking.

Eve tossed her bag onto the sofa and plowed her fingers through her hair. It was almost dry now, but it smelled like nasty harbor water. "There's a change of clothes in the bedroom." She nodded toward his arm. "You should probably shower and clean up that wound. I'll make some coffee."

He looked around the room. It was the perfect get-away. That was why she'd chosen it. The small but upscale kitchen with an intimate dining spot included a magnificent view of the trees and mountains surrounding them. A cozy living room with a fireplace—not that they would need it in July—comfy leather furniture, no distractions. No television, no VCR, no radio. Just a CD player with a collection of let's-make-love music. And wine. She had made sure there was wine and food, along with a couple of changes of clothes. She knew his size…by heart.

"Then," he said, that dark gaze colliding with hers, "I'm going to ask questions and you're going to answer them. All of them."

He gave her his back and headed for the only other room in the cabin: the bedroom suite. Jacuzzi tub, a shower large enough to dance in. And a massive king-size bed surrounded by floor-to-ceiling windows.

Not exactly your regular, everyday cabin.

This one was designed and furnished for making memories.

The forever kind.

Eve hadn't made a forever kind of memory in her entire life.

Starting now would be a mistake.

J.T. PEELED THE BANDAGE from his biceps. Winced. A little bleeding from the physical exertion in the water, but he'd live.

He tossed the soiled bandage into the trash and stared at his reflection in the mirror. What the hell had Eve gotten herself into?

The better question was, what the hell was he doing in the middle of it?

He braced his hands on the counter and closed his eyes against the light. The water was running in the shower but it would have to wait. He badly needed to pull himself together here. She'd drugged him. He didn't have to confirm his suspicion. The grogginess and slowed reactions were confirmation enough.

He'd lost an entire day of his life. That much he'd figured out. Ian had dropped him off at his place last night, technically night before last, since it was past midnight. Someone had attacked him in his own house. He remembered absolutely nothing after that until he woke up in the warehouse.

J.T. opened his eyes and grimaced as he rubbed the back of his head. If she had planned to drug him, why whack him on the head?

Just another question he intended to ask.

He kicked off his shoes and stripped off his clothes. His arm ached with the effort. Stepping into the shower, he embraced the hot water, which felt good pounding his flesh. He stood there and let it pour over him for a while. Until his tense muscles relaxed a bit.

Those moments when her lips had sealed across his kept replaying in his mind. He'd missed her so much, even when he'd learned she wasn't who he thought she was. The need to touch her again, to see her, still thrived in his veins—however hard he'd attempted to squelch the lingering need. Those long blond tresses…her toned body…and those blue eyes.

He shook his head, hating the fact that she could still make him want her so badly.

He didn't even know who she was…where she'd come from…nothing.

She'd fooled him, used him for purposes still unknown to him.

This woman had stolen his firm grip on reality.

He needed answers.

Making fast work of washing his hair and his body, he quickly mentally prioritized the numerous questions he intended to ask.

As soon as he had his answers, he was out of here.

Whatever her game or her troubles, he would not be a part of any of it.

She could find some other guy to play the part of fool.

When he'd dried his skin, he checked out the clothes she'd supplied. Underwear. Socks. She'd planned this whole thing down to the last detail. The idea made him mad as hell all over again.

She'd said this was about him, but unless it involved the Colby Agency, it couldn't possibly have anything to do with him.

He needed to contact the agency as soon as possible and bring them up to speed as to his whereabouts. He'd missed the all-hands briefing. Victoria would be wondering what had happened to him. The abduction attempt had been particularly hard on her.

If he discovered that *this* had anything to do with Victoria or her granddaughter, Eve would seriously regret the day she'd gotten involved with whoever was behind the Colby Agency's troubles.

J.T. pulled on the boxers and jeans, then the T-shirt. He checked his biceps. No more bleeding. Another bandage would be nice, but—

A tap on the door jerked his attention in that direction. He plowed his fingers through his hair, took a breath, then opened the door.

She still wore the damp cami and jeans. Her hair was mostly dry. It hung around her shoulders as if she'd just awakened from a long night of...

Stop. Don't go there.

"I thought you might need this." She held out a

first aid kit. "It's a habit of mine." She shrugged. "I always keep one in my vehicle."

He stared at the kit as he accepted it, then lifted his gaze to hers. "Seems you have a lot of habits I didn't know about."

She held his gaze a moment before walking away without comment.

Maybe she had a conscience after all.

Nah…he doubted it.

When he'd covered his stitches with a fresh bandage, he cleaned up the mess he'd made and headed for the showdown. His gut growled—his appetite had reappeared full force.

He would have some answers first.

Unable to help himself, he paused at the foot of the sprawling bed. They were supposed to have had their honeymoon night here. Images of making love—fingers fisted in all that gorgeous hair of hers…sheets tangled around long, toned legs— flashed like a seductive preview in his mind.

His heart pounded with the memories.

Yes, he was an infinite fool.

He stalked out of the room.

"I made you a sandwich." She gestured to the bar that separated the living room from the small kitchen. "Ham and cheese with mayo, your favorite."

Anger simmered in his gut, replacing the need for

food. Yeah, she knew all his favorites. His likes and dislikes. She knew everything because he'd been honest with her, and he knew nothing about her.

Because she'd lied.

About everything.

"For the third time," he said, his voice low and hard, "who are you?"

She picked up her plate and got comfortable on the sofa. "That's a tough one." Her long fingers tore off a chunk of sandwich. He watched with far too much interest as she lifted it to those lush lips.

The anger started to boil. The games ended now. "It's an easy question. What's your real name? The one you were given at birth."

"The name on a birth certificate is irrelevant in all the ways that matter." She moved her shoulders in a display of indifference. "My name's Eve. Eve Mattson. I'm twenty-nine. I live at—"

"Lincoln Park, 2209 Pratt Street." He plopped into the chair across from her position. "That's all crap. I checked. You've had numerous aliases in the past six or seven years. But that's as far back as I could trace you. As far as records are concerned, you didn't exist at all before that."

Even as he said the words, the whole situation didn't feel real. Felt impossible. How could he have fallen in love with all the…lies? With a woman who didn't exist? The better question was, how could he have been so blind?

She dropped her bare feet to the carpeted floor and set her plate on the coffee table. With her forearms braced on her spread knees, she looked him dead in the eye. "The truth is I don't even remember who I was…before. I am who you see at the moment. That changes when the need arises."

A frown pulled at his forehead. "Don't snow me. Where were you born? Who were your parents? Where'd you go to school?"

"I need wine." She stood, stretched, then walked over to the bar and poured a glass of the red wine she'd already uncorked.

He waited, his frustration mounting rapidly as she resettled on the sofa. "I'm waiting." He wasn't having anything less than the whole truth. And he wasn't going to keep playing these guessing games.

She stretched again. The cami tightened on her breasts. He looked away.

"Arizona."

His attention returned to her.

"Phoenix, Arizona." She downed half the glass of wine, licked her lips and stared straight into his eyes. "But that girl doesn't exist anymore. I am Eve Matt-son. So move on to the next question."

Fury tightened his jaw. "What kind of con are you

running?" The admission reminded him that he'd been an even bigger fool than he'd known. What was in this for her?

"This isn't a con, J.T." She cradled her glass, stroked it with the pad of her thumb. That he noticed only made him angrier. "You're in danger and I'm trying to save you."

Laughter burst from his chest. He'd heard it all now. She was trying to *save* him? "You whack me on the back of the head. Drug me," he said pointedly, "and kidnap me. Now you're telling me you're trying to save me?" He laughed again. "From whom? Your associates?" His gaze narrowed. "Or from you?"

The last of her wine disappeared. "You keep trying to make this about me, J.T."

He shot to his feet, shook his head and paid the price as pain erupted all over again. "This is about you, Eve." Just saying her name made his gut clench. Fury bolted through him.

She moved her head slowly from side to side. "No, J.T." She pushed up, walked back to where the bottle of wine sat and poured herself a second glass. "This has nothing to do with me." She leaned against the counter and pursed her lips. "Well, I suppose now it does. But it didn't start out that way."

"Tell me the truth," he bit out the words. "The whole truth. Starting from the beginning. From the day you crashed into my life." Literally. She'd rearended him. No real damage to either car, more a fender-bender.

That blue gaze coupled with his. "It started with a job." One shoulder lifted in the slightest shrug. "Seemed simple enough at the time. But, as you can see, everything's changed now."

He held her gaze, waited for her to continue.

"Now they want you dead…. And my conscience won't let me just walk away."

Chapter Six

"Who wants me dead?"

Eve pushed off the counter and reclaimed her seat on the sofa. "That's the problem." She sipped the wine. "I don't know who. If I did, I would have taken care of the situation already." This mystery was wrapped in numerous layers.

More of that frustration etched across J.T.'s handsome face. "You have to know who hired you and the goal of the assignment."

It was never that simple. "Three months ago I was contacted through my Web site."

A frown furrowed his brow. "What Web site?"

Before she could answer one question, he came up with another. "Problemsolver.com—that's me. Clients leave their contact numbers. I do a background search first to weed out the feds and P.I.s, then call and interview each legitimate client. I determine if I'm interested in the job and go from there."

J.T. motioned for her to continue. His expression, his every move, was steeped in distrust and frustration. That shouldn't bother her, but it did. She had allowed herself to get way too close to this guy.

Dangerously close.

"Like I was saying," she went on, "three months ago I was contacted by a male who called himself 'the Auditor.' When I refused to discuss his proposition without a real name, he gave me the name Terrence Arenas."

"Arenas?" J.T.'s frown deepened. "Terrence Arenas is a fraud investigator at Gold Coast Life. We worked together for years. He retired right before I moved to the Colby Agency."

"That's right. Arenas indicated to me that he had a situation. A problem he needed solved." This was where things would get hairy. "Before he retired he ripped off about ten mil from GCL."

"That's not possible," J.T. argued. "There are far too many checks and balances."

He hesitated. Eve watched realization dawn on his face.

"Unless," J.T. qualified, "he had a partner who was a beneficiary."

"Paula Jamison."

"I verified that case myself." J.T. stood, braced his hands on his hips. "There was some question about the beneficiary, Paula Jamison, but that was cleared up. The payment was made. End of story."

"You met Ms. Jamison?"

He nodded, then strode to the front window to stare out at the darkness. She knew what he was doing. He was mentally reviewing the case, confirming what he thought to be the truth.

"That must be the reason Arenas wants you dead now."

J.T. turned back to face her but remained near the window. "That makes absolutely no sense. Arenas had nothing to do with the Jamison case."

"All I know is," she reiterated, "he hired me to find out if you'd kept any documentation on the case. Or if you were investigating it in any way. Or any others, for that matter."

"It took you two months to make and confirm a determination?"

She moistened her lips. Dread swelled in her throat. "It wasn't until a few days before…the wedding…that you gave me access to your most private files. Being thorough is important to my reputation."

He turned away and stared out the window once more.

A week before their scheduled wedding, he'd

given her full access to everything in his home, his bank account…everything. She'd confirmed what she had pretty much already known, and then she'd disappeared.

Because the job was over.

Or she'd thought it was.

"So hitting my SUV was no accident."

He swung around once more. His gaze bored into hers. All emotion had vanished from his face, disappeared from his tone.

"No accident." No point in lying. He already understood that she'd deceived him. "It was an entry strategy." The words left a sour taste in her mouth. She'd never once—never—had second thoughts or regrets about a job.

But this one was different.

"Once you had what you wanted—" he moved back to the chair, settled into it "—why'd you come back? Even if what you say about Arenas is true, there's no reason for him to want me dead."

She shook her head. "I can't tell you why he wants you dead. All I know is that's what he wants. He, or someone claiming to be him, contacted me four days ago for the debrief and finalization of payment. When our conversation concluded, he hung up but some glitch or oversight prevented the call from being disconnected. I overheard him tell a colleague that he didn't care that I had confirmed you were not a threat—he wanted you dead anyway. I've been watching you ever since. Night before last, you were supposed to die. You would come home and there would be a fire. Too bad for you."

"How is it you knew the intruder's precise intentions?"

"I had a little chat in your living room with the intruder who cracked you on the head. He was all too happy to talk, in hopes of gaining immunity."

"Did you kill him?"

She inclined her head but kept her gaze steady on his. "Yes. I had no choice. He made a dive for my weapon." That was true. Though letting him go wouldn't have been a good move in either case. Maybe the guy had sensed she was leaning in a direction that wasn't in his best interest.

"Why are we here?" Suspicion lit in his eyes now. "It appears you do know who the enemy is. Why all the subterfuge? If what you say is true, why wouldn't I just go to the police? Take Arenas down?"

"Arenas is dead. His body was discovered five days ago."

The frown was back. "You said you'd spoken to him four days ago."

"I said I'd spoken to a man who claimed to be Arenas. The man I'd been dealing with, obviously, wasn't Arenas. Particularly since Arenas had been missing for more than two weeks before his body was discovered. The man retired and then he goes missing. Sounds fishy to me."

"Then we look to his presumed partner, Paula Jamison."

"Also dead," Eve let him know. "She died just over three months ago."

THIS NEWS STUNNED J.T. Anytime that two people involved with the transfer of this much money died within a few weeks of each other, suspicion was aroused.

Coincidence…maybe.

Worthy of looking into…definitely.

J.T. had known Terrence Arenas for four years. He was an older man nearing retirement, and J.T. hadn't sensed even the slightest hint of deception in his nature. Someone else had to be behind this initiative.

Whatever the hell it was.

For now, all he had were the details provided by a woman who'd already betrayed him in the most basic way. He damned sure wasn't taking her word for anything.

The fact that they had been shot at and chased proved there was trouble, but whether or not it actually involved J.T. or his previous employer was yet to be seen.

J.T. had no reason to believe there had been any underhanded dealings in the Jamison case. He certainly hadn't noted any deception when the beneficiary payment was executed. Nor had he noted any reason to be suspicious after the fact.

The better part of a year later, he couldn't fathom that whatever Eve was involved with had anything to do with the Jamison case—or with him, for that matter.

But he didn't take kindly to having his home invaded, being abducted, shot at or chased.

"What was Arenas's cause of death?" If the man died of natural causes, that would certainly shed a different light on the situation.

"I tapped into the coroner's database and—"

"You tapped into the coroner's database?" Who the hell was this woman?

He'd asked that question many times already.

"It's not that complicated," she countered, "as I'm sure you're aware."

It wasn't. Not for those with the proper skills and the predilection for the illegal. J.T. simply couldn't get past the idea that this was the woman he'd fallen in love with…had intended to marry.

"The final autopsy report is not available as of

yet," she explained, "but the preliminary assessment is that foul play was involved in his death."

"And what about Paula Jamison?"

"Automobile accident. Brake failure."

J.T. scrubbed a hand over his chin. Was it possible someone in the insurance agency had been exploiting clients? Or working some other scam?

An investigation was assuredly in order.

But J.T. had other obligations he would need to square away first. "I'll need to check in with my current employer," he warned the woman sitting across from him. "Then, I'll need to do some digging of my own."

"I'm afraid the former is impossible." She pushed out of her chair and wandered back to the bar. Rather than pouring herself another drink, she picked at the sandwich she'd made for him since he hadn't touched it.

J.T. shook his head and got to his feet. "You can't keep me here against my will any more than you can prevent me from making a phone call."

She reached into her back pocket and pulled out her cell phone. "This is the only phone for miles." She popped a bit of cheese into her mouth, chewed a couple of times, then swallowed. "The keys to the only car around and my Glock are hidden."

"Walking hasn't gone out of style." He headed

for the door. He wasn't playing by her rules. If she wanted to dig out her gun, more power to her.

He was finished.

"J.T."

He hesitated at the door, his hand already on the knob. He shouldn't have, but there was something in her voice. An uncertainty…a fragility almost…that he hadn't heard before.

"If you go, they won't stop until you're dead. Trust me on this. This man, whoever the hell he is, is not playing."

He turned back, allowed his gaze to connect with hers. "I'm a big boy, Eve. I can take care of myself. I was doing it long before I met you."

As he reached for the dead bolt, she spoke again. "This is my responsibility."

He stilled as she moved closer.

He should have flipped that latch.

Should have walked out the door.

"I suppose if I hadn't taken the job, someone else would've. But that doesn't lessen the responsibility I feel. I…I don't want to leave you in this position. I want to finish this…the right way."

"You already finished it, Eve."

She placed a hand on his arm. The warmth of her soft skin premeated into him, made him weak when he needed to be strong.

"We're finished—I understand that. You'll never trust me again. And you shouldn't. I'm not a trustworthy person. But this job…this guy is not finished by a long shot. He needs to ensure you're out of the way, for whatever his twisted, selfish reasons are. He needs to be stopped. That's the thing I have to finish before I go."

He turned his head just far enough to make eye contact. The urge to laugh at the sincerity in her eyes was very nearly overwhelming. How did she expect him to trust her words when everything about her was a lie?

"You've done your job. It's time for you to move on to the next job. You don't owe me anything. You can walk away with a clear conscience. I'm not your fiancé or lover. I'm not even your friend."

She flinched. Actually flinched for the second time since he'd awakened in that warehouse.

His heart reacted.

He wasn't sure which of them was the bigger fool.

Maybe they both were fools.

"Give me twenty-four hours," she asked. This was her second request for time. "If I haven't proved useful to your efforts by then, I'll be on my way."

He shouldn't change his mind. "I have to contact the Colby Agency."

"I live by one firm rule, J.T., and it's gotten me

through until now." She made a sound, a sort of laugh, but it was glaringly lacking in humor. "And believe me, I've been in some seriously tight spots. The motto that's gotten me through those spots is trust no one. No outside contact whatsoever until this is done."

She just didn't understand the Colby Agency. That was the one place on this planet where complete trust not only existed but also thrived.

"Twenty-four hours," he repeated. He supposed contacting the agency could wait. The first chance he got, he would make the call. She couldn't keep an eye on him every minute.

She nodded. "Twenty-four hours."

He shrugged. "After the swim we took, your phone probably doesn't work anyway." He hadn't considered that until just now. He obviously should have.

Eve smiled. "I never leave anything to chance, J.T. I keep a spare cell phone in my car." She tucked the phone into her back pocket once more. "I don't know how we ever survived without them."

How the hell had he missed this level of shrewdness? Then another thought zinged him. "Are you suggesting I stay *here*—" he glanced back at the door leading to the one bedroom "—with you?"

She paused, as if considering the question. "I'll take the couch," she offered. "No problem."

He had to be out of his mind.

"Tomorrow morning we go see whoever survived Paula Jamison." He would be in charge of where they went from here. No negotiations.

"Absolutely. As soon as I learned that detail, I checked into who her beneficiary was. Leonard Jamison. A brother. He's her only surviving family."

"We'll do this my way," he spelled out, just to be sure she understood him.

She held her hands up. "I have no problem with that."

He knew that one thing about her if he knew nothing else—no way would she play the loyal soldier. She liked having input far too much.

"As long," she added, "as we play by my rules."

"I guess we'll just have to work that out as we go."

Oh, yeah. He was definitely off his rocker.

Here he was with the woman who'd vanished on their wedding day. In the very place they had been scheduled to spend their honeymoon night.

And he hadn't a clue who she really was.

Chapter Seven

6:15 a.m.

J.T. awoke with a jerk.

For a moment he felt disoriented.

Sunlight bled through the narrowed slits of the blinds. The sights and sounds around him were unfamiliar. He blinked and reality crowded in on his chest.

Eve.

He was with Eve. At the cabin.

Sitting upright, he glanced around the room, listening intently. Movement in the next room. Barely audible. The scent of freshly brewed coffee wafted into the room even as he struggled to gain his bearings.

She was up already.

His attention shifted to the telephone on the bedside table. She'd disabled the three phones in the cabin before they'd arrived. Though she'd slept on the couch, as offered, he'd sensed her presence at the bedroom door at regular intervals throughout the morning hours. Checking on him. He would have done the same if their situations were reversed.

The residue of the drug she'd given him had ensured he slept, albeit fitfully. He doubted she'd slept at all. More likely to assure he didn't go anywhere than because she was worried about him.

He threw the cover back and dropped his socked feet to the floor. He'd slept in his clothes. Part of him had considered making a run for it. He wasn't concerned that she would actually use the Glock.

But, his need to understand what was really going down had kept him here.

That decision could prove another mistake, but he'd made the choice. There was no need for second thoughts now.

He made a pit stop in the bathroom, ran his fingers through his hair and then went in search of his host, or captor, depending on how one looked at the situation. His need to check in with the Colby Agency nagged at him, but he pushed it aside for the moment.

When this was done, Victoria would understand his choice.

He hoped she and her granddaughter were still safe. By now, Victoria may have been forced to contact her son and daughter-in-law—if they were reachable. Vacationing in the wilds of Africa made one unreachable to some degree. The idea that gunfire had been exchanged in the confrontation Friday night meant the situation had escalated to one of a lethal nature. No amount of security would protect Victoria or her grandchild if the enemy persisted. Mistakes, oversights and mere off days were had by all. The elite staff of the Colby Agency was no different.

And it took only one mistake, one oversight…one distracted moment.

The child's parents would need to be informed—if possible.

J.T. followed the luring scent of coffee into the main room. Evidently Eve had decided he was in a deep enough sleep to risk taking a shower. Her long hair was damp. His mind instantly conjured images of her naked body in that massive shower. Just as quickly flashes of him joining her, pulling her body to his in a frantic sex session, inserted themselves into the mix.

He gritted his teeth and banished the images.

Never again.

They might be wary allies for the moment, but he would never again trust her.

Or be vulnerable to her.

They were done.

"There's cereal," she announced. "And coffee. I'm sure you're hungry by now."

A long pause elapsed while he went momentarily stupid. She'd turned to face him and those big blue eyes had captured him as surely as if she'd shoved that Glock of hers in his face.

Stupid, J.T. Really stupid.

"I'm fine." He wasn't—his stomach grumbled in protest. But he wasn't eating anything she prepared, not after she'd drugged him once already.

Still, his gaze lingered on the carafe. She poured herself a cup and took a cautious sip.

"Hmm." She lifted her cup to him. "I might not be much of a cook, but I can make coffee."

He snagged a cup and filled it with the hot brew. The smell alone had his mouth watering. He couldn't deny that the woman knew how to make coffee.

When he'd downed enough caffeine to make him feel remotely human, he reluctantly made himself a bowl of cereal, then got down to business. "We should get moving." Staying in one place under the circumstances wouldn't be a good idea.

"I'm ready." She set her cup aside and hit the off button on the coffeemaker.

He finished his cereal and coffee, then went in search of his shoes. Unfortunately they were still wet, but they'd have to do. Though she'd had the foresight to stock clothes and food, shoes hadn't been on her list. But then again, he doubted that taking a swim in the harbor had been on her original agenda.

"Ready?"

The question brought him up short. How many times had she asked him that when they were living together? She always managed to be prepared before him for work or a leisurely outing.

He had to stop getting distracted by flashes from the past. Eve Mattson was not the woman he'd thought he knew. She was a stranger.

Right now had nothing to do with last month.

They were strangers attempting to survive…and to get the bad guy.

Nothing more.

EVE LET HIM DRIVE. She figured it would be easier to keep an eye on him if she wasn't preoccupied with maneuvering from point A to point B.

On some level that had been a bad decision, she decided as they reached the rural community of Green Oaks, twenty or so miles outside of Chicago. Since she wasn't distracted by traffic or road signs, she was left with the irresistible chore of analyzing every visible inch of J.T. She'd tried to avoid giving in, but the feat had been impossible.

She'd loved looking at his profile when they were

together. Classic square jaw, perfectly symmetrical nose. And his hair. He had the greatest hair. Dark, dark brown—almost black. Just like his eyes. But, she had to admit, that his lips were his best asset by far. Full for a man's. Amazingly talented in the art of kissing.

When she wasn't able to bear studying that handsome profile any longer, she got lost just looking at his hands. Square hands, long fingers—blunt tipped like a guitar player's. The memory of feeling those hands on her body all those nights they'd made love warmed her skin even now…even knowing that he despised her for what she'd done…for who she was.

She blinked, told herself to look away but couldn't resist, following the hand to the wrist…along the muscular forearm and biceps.

He was staring straight at her.

She jumped. Gasped.

"Which way?" he asked.

He'd stopped at an intersection. She was supposed to be providing directions.

"Sorry. Right. Take a right here."

Incredibly, her cheeks were flaming with embarrassment.

She straightened in her seat and stared at the road. The next turn would be coming up soon. Mr. Jamison lived on a small farm he and his sister had inherited from their parents.

"The next left," she said, this time giving J.T. ample warning.

Okay, pull it together, girl. Focus on the task at hand. Nothing else was real.

Never had been.

J.T. slowed for the turn.

"Mr. Jamison is sixty-eight and physically disabled. He rarely leaves home."

"You've met him?" J.T. glanced at her as he made that final turn.

She shook her head. "No. That was in the background search."

The gravel road leading to the farm was rutted and in need of attention. As the house came into view, Eve wondered what would make a woman who'd gotten a multimillion dollar insurance payout for her husband's death stay in a place like this.

J.T. parked in front of the house. "You're sure this is the place?"

He'd likely had the same thought she had. "This is it."

The place looked deserted. No vehicles around. The white farmhouse wasn't in such bad shape. It had been painted fairly recently and looked in good repair. Two stories. Picket fence around the yard. The woods surrounding the property came right up to the backyard, providing privacy and atmosphere.

She opened the car door and climbed out. Quiet. Really quiet.

Too quiet.

The possibility that the enemy had gotten here first rammed her in the gut.

Scanning the property, she made her way to the porch. J.T. stayed close behind her. The silence was unnerving. Jamison lived alone. It was early on a Sunday morning. He could still be in bed.

The screen door creaked as she opened it. She pounded hard on the wood door. If he was in there, she wanted him to hear her.

The warmth of J.T.'s body so close behind hers temporarily distracted her from the silence radiating all around them.

She banged on the door again. *Focus*. Thinking about him or his body was a bad idea.

Labored footsteps approaching the door drew her back to full attention. Someone was home. Good. Hopefully it would be the man they sought.

The door opened with the same kind of aged creak as the screen door had. A small, rotund man with a crown of gray hair peered out at her.

"You from the church?" he asked, his tone something less than pleased.

"Mr. Jamison?" she inquired. "Leonard Jamison?"

"That's right." He scratched his head. "I told them

folks that stopped by the other day that I don't usually get up and around early enough on Sunday morning to go to no services."

"We're not from the church, Mr. Jamison," Eve explained. "May we come in? We'd like to speak to you regarding your sister, Paula."

His bushy gray eyebrows knitted in confusion. "She passed away a few months ago, you know."

"Yes, sir," Eve said patiently. "That's one of the things we wanted to discuss with you."

She felt herself holding her breath as he considered her request.

"Well, all right. I guess." He shuffled back from the door.

Eve opened the screen door wider and stepped inside, careful to keep her movements unhurried and unthreatening.

"Thank you, Mr. Jamison." She covertly surveyed the room. Cluttered. Old furnishings. Not ragged or dirty, just old. "We appreciate your time."

"What'd you say your name was?" he asked as he shuffled to a well-worn chair.

"I'm Christina Allison." She crossed to where he sat and offered her hand. "And this is my colleague Charles Wentz." The man shook her hand; his was cool and frail. "We're from the review board. We're here about your sister's accident."

Jamison gestured to the sofa. "Have a seat, then. I don't know why you're back here. You said there wasn't nothing wrong with the car. The mechanic said otherwise."

Eve exchanged a look with J.T.

"Mr. Jamison," J.T. offered, "we don't represent the auto manufacturer. Why don't we review what you've been told so far regarding the accident?"

Jamison shrugged his rounded shoulders. "Police said her brakes failed. The mechanic said it was some kind of defect. The manufacturer sent their own mechanic, and he said that wasn't so. The part that failed wasn't original to the car. Said whoever worked on it last messed something up."

"Did your mechanic work on the car prior to the accident?" Eve prodded.

Jamison shook his head. "Never had it worked on. It was too new to need working on."

The sister had a new car. So maybe she had spent some of the settlement money.

"Killed her instantly, they said," Jamison went on. "Roads was slick. She hit a tree." He waved a hand. "She wasn't no fast driver. Didn't make a whole lot of sense to me, but I'm just an old man."

Eve moistened her lips. So far the old gentleman didn't seem to mind talking about his deceased sister, but they were about to broach sensitive territory.

"You're the only beneficiary of your sister's estate?" That was the gentlest way she knew to ask.

He nodded. "Wasn't that much to it." He looked around the room. "This old farm our folks left. The insurance money from the wrecked car. Enough to give her a decent burial."

Another of those looks passed between J.T. and Eve. That didn't make a whole hell of a lot of sense.

"Mr. Jamison," J.T. began, "I know these questions are of a sensitive nature. But it's very important that we understand every aspect of the final year and a half of your sister's life."

Jamison's gaze held J.T.'s long enough for Eve to get antsy. If he clammed up now, they might not get the answers they needed most.

"Ask what you come here to ask, Mr. Wentz. I don't imagine I've got a whole lot more living to do, but what I got left would be a good bit more peaceful if I knew what really happened to my sister."

"Were you aware of any dealings your sister might have had with Terrence Arenas from Gold Coast Life?"

Mr. Jamison harrumphed. "She had some dealings with him, all right. Him and that company beat her out of what she was entitled to."

J.T. glanced at Eve before continuing. "According to the company's records, your sister received a payment of two million dollars for her husband's death."

Jamison shook his head, his face scrunched with what looked like anger. "That's what she was supposed to get, rightly enough. But she didn't get it. That thief Arenas said that the autopsy showed that Paula's husband smoked. His policy listed him as a nonsmoker. Paula was offered a settlement of fifty thousand dollars. Arenas said that was coming from the goodness of his heart."

"You're certain—" Eve jumped in "—that her dealings on the matter were with Mr. Arenas?"

Jamison nodded. "She cursed him enough times. I don't think I'll be forgetting that name anytime soon."

"Did you ever meet him?" J.T. asked. "Perhaps he visited your sister here?"

Another shake of his gray head. "If he'd come here, I might've been tempted to shoot him."

"Is there any way," J.T. pressed, "that your sister may have gotten the two million dollars and you didn't know?"

Jamison leaned forward. "Listen here," he growled, "I watched my sister cry over her dead husband. Who didn't smoke, by the way. Then I watched her lose her home and have to come back here and live with me because she couldn't pay the mortgage payments without her husband's income or the insurance. What little insurance she got was spent on his medical expenses and burying him. I think I know what happened."

When J.T. didn't argue, the old man added, "She was cheated by that bastard Arenas. Don't you doubt it for a second. That man and his company killed my sister."

"You believe," Eve ventured, "that the stress of all that happened caused her death?"

A weary hazel-eyed gaze settled on hers. "No, ma'am, that's not what I believe at all. My sister told 'em she was getting herself a lawyer. It took me nearly a year, but I finally talked her into it. She called up Arenas and told him what she was gonna do. And then she was dead. They killed her as sure as I live and breathe."

Eve stood. She'd heard enough to be convinced. "Thank you, Mr. Jamison. We'll let you know the results as soon as we've completed our investigation."

"Just make sure Arenas pays," the old man insisted. "That's all I care about now."

J.T. made similar assurances to the man as he and Eve departed. He made no comments as to his thoughts until they were in the car and driving away.

"There's one way to verify Jamison's story."

That he needed verification told Eve that J.T. wasn't completely convinced of his former colleague's guilt. He needed tangible evidence.

"How's that?" Might as well go with the flow.

She needed him to see this for what it was—a threat to his survival.

"We have someone inside the company dig around until they find the record of the actual payments. What I approved was the order for the payments but not the actual checks."

"If that person's still alive," Eve countered.

J.T. sent her a questioning look.

"This is a cleanup detail," she explained to the man who clearly wanted to believe the best of his former employer. "The killing won't stop until anyone who's a threat is eliminated."

"You can't be certain," J.T. argued. "This could be an isolated situation. Besides, Arenas is already dead. He may have been the only threat—assuming he was guilty."

"All that means is that he had a partner," Eve insisted. Why didn't he just admit that his former employer was dirty?

"Those guys last night may have been about my work at the Colby Agency or a previous job of yours. We don't know that any of this is related."

Eve wanted to laugh, but it wasn't funny at all. "What I know is," she said instead, "that the sooner you accept the truth, the greater your odds of staying alive."

She wanted this done so she could blow this town.

She'd thought this part wouldn't be a problem.

But she'd been wrong.

She didn't want to spend any more time than was necessary with J.T.

Looking at him, drawing in his scent with every breath, was harder than she'd expected.

She should just let him take it from here.

"I think we have a tail."

She craned her neck to check out the vehicle coming upon their car's rear bumper entirely too fast.

"I think you're—"

Her words stalled as she recognized the other driver's intent. "He's going to—"

The car rammed into their rear bumper.

Chapter Eight

Chicago, 10:00 a.m.

"Please, sit down, Ian." Victoria settled on her sofa, but her nerves were anything but. Ian had news or he wouldn't have arrived at her home on a Sunday morning.

Ian lowered his tall frame onto the sofa. His dark eyes showed the weariness of the past week. With Lucas, her greatly missed husband, still out of pocket, Ian felt personally responsible for Victoria's and Jamie's safety. Ian had been with her at the Colby Agency the longest. Her son, Jim, and his wife, Tasha, trusted Ian implicitly. He would want Ian in charge of his daughter's safety.

Jamie was in the den watching a movie with Merrilee Walters, the newest member of the Colby Agency staff. Jamie had taken to the young woman immediately. A former schoolteacher, Merri loved children. Jamie was fiercely intrigued by the fact that Merri was deaf. She didn't precisely understand the lipreading concept quite yet, but she loved learning to sign.

"Simon is following up on the leads related to the Blackstone Firm," Ian began.

The Blackstone Firm had traditionally been the Colby Agency's strongest competition. Robert Blackstone had been a fine man who'd built a firm based on integrity. After his death, three years ago, his son had decided that fame and fortune would be the foundation of the firm. Integrity had gone out the proverbial window.

"I," Ian continued, "have been attempting to track down J.T."

The idea that J.T. was still missing concerned Victoria greatly. The longer the lack of communication continued, the higher the risk that his life was at stake. "Still no word from him?"

"I'm afraid not. However, there is a development."

Victoria braced herself. Judging by Ian's tone, the news was not good.

"While reviewing his personal files, hard copy as well as electronic, we've discovered a numbered account for a bank in Grand Cayman. There appears to be a very large sum of money in the account. The account is fairly new, with a rather large deposit made about two months ago. Since there is no known legitimate source for the income, not to mention the account itself raises a red flag, there is reason for concern."

"How large?" Victoria was not prepared to judge J.T. on this evidence. She knew him too well. If an overseas account containing a large sum of money was connected to his name, it was either a mistake or a lifetime's savings. Perhaps an insurance residual from his father's death.

"Half a million."

J.T.'s family was wealthy by no means. To have amassed such a sum…it simply wasn't possible. There had to be another explanation.

"What about insurance?" Victoria offered. "His father's death may have provided a large insurance benefit."

"That's the first possibility I checked," Ian explained. "The sum was minimal."

Victoria squared her shoulders. "Any additional findings?" Ian was a brilliant investigator. There was no need for her to question his findings. He would not stop until he had the real story.

"None yet. There's been no activity on any of J.T.'s credit cards or his ATM card. His cell phone has been turned off, so the attempt to track his whereabouts that way was futile. His vehicle remains untouched."

Victoria prayed he was not dead. Having to pass along the news that he was missing had been hard enough on his mother. She'd lost her husband, J.T.'s father, only last year. Victoria knew all too well that emotional burden. She wasn't sure his mother could survive losing J.T., too.

"Contact me the moment you learn anything new," Victoria urged.

"Of course." Ian stood. "Jane will replace Merrilee at seven."

"Thank you, Ian." Victoria rose and saw him to the door. "I'm certain your children are missing their father." Ian had worked around the clock for the past several days. He would not rest until the threat to Victoria was neutralized. Yet, he and his wife, Nicole, had two lovely children, he was needed at home, too.

"Nicole has things under control," he assured Victoria. He hesitated before leaving. "I'll continue to rotate two investigators on exterior security duty in six-hour shifts. We'll keep the interior security on twelve hours."

Victoria nodded. It was easier on Jamie if the changing faces inside were limited to two within a twenty-four-hour period. Both Merrilee Walters and Jane Sutton were good with the child. Jane had grown up in a large family and loved playing games with Jamie.

Again, Ian hesitated.

"Is there something more?" Victoria had never known him to be less than blunt with whatever was on his mind. But he seemed reluctant to some degree today. The hesitation sent her anxiety to an even higher level.

"A name from Jim's past has surfaced in this puzzling mix."

A trickling of fear made Victoria's pulse skip erratically. Whatever the name, it would not be good. Jim's past was littered with unsavory characters. She searched Ian's eyes for some measure of the gravity of this disclosure. "What name?"

"Bear in mind," Ian said carefully, "that the connection we've discovered appears to be only in the vaguest of terms. But I could not ignore the marker. Particularly this one."

"The name, Ian," Victoria prompted. "What is the name?"

"Errol Leberman."

Impossible. "Leberman is dead." Victoria's voice sounded empty…cold. Her chest felt the same. There had to be a mistake. The only other logical conclusion was that someone was using the name to get to Victoria.

It worked.

Leberman had been the archenemy of her first husband, James Colby. He had murdered her first husband and had abducted and brutalized their son in ways that still haunted her. The bastard had been twisted and pure evil.

"I'm certain," Ian assured, "this is a ruse to confuse the investigation. But I cannot ignore the possibility that someone close to him has decided to take up the cause."

"Do whatever you have to," Victoria agreed, her head starting to spin.

"I would strongly recommend that you attempt to contact Lucas again. He should be made aware of this development."

Leberman had tried to destroy everything Victoria loved. His goal had been to wipe out the Colby Agency and all that it stood for.

But he'd failed.

He was dead.

Victoria had insisted on confirming that fact with her own eyes.

But his evil deeds and that sinister name lived on, it appeared.

Chapter Nine

J.T. wrestled the car back under control.

"He's coming again!"

As J.T. braced for a second assault, Eve dug into her bag for her Glock.

"If they wanted us dead," J.T. warned, "we would likely already be that way."

"You think?" Eve released her seat belt and turned to level an aim out the rear window.

He'd been analyzing the recent run-in. Whoever these guys were, they hadn't worked too hard at terminating their targets. "Those shots the other night went pretty wide. Five guys shooting and no one gets a hit? Doesn't sound like the kind of professionals I know."

"What about the guy who ambushed you at your house?" Eve grabbed hold of the headrest to brace herself. "Here they come."

The sedan rammed their rear bumper a second

time, harder this time. The car jolted forward and careened dangerously on the curvy road.

J.T. wrangled back control and floored the accelerator.

"He whacked me on the head," J.T. said in answer to her question. "He didn't shoot me. He could've done far worse."

"He damned sure would've shot me," Eve argued.

"Maybe he needs me alive."

"Whatever." She wasn't ready to agree. "Let's just lose these guys, okay?"

"Let's."

J.T. wasn't familiar with the area, so he allowed Eve to make the decisions on directions.

"Take the next right."

"You might want to buckle up." He waited until the last possible moment and hit the brakes hard, then made an even harder right.

The sedan, close on their tail, missed the turn entirely.

Eve slid back into her seat and fastened her seat belt. "The next left. There's a long, curvy stretch after that. Very little traffic. If you keep it floored, they won't catch up."

He took the left, scarcely slowing down at all. The tires squealed. The rear of the car fishtailed. He straightened it out and rammed the accelerator.

The car lunged forward, the momentum pressing his back into the seat.

"Still clear." Eve kept an eye on the side mirror so J.T. could focus on the road.

The speedometer topped out; he kept pushing the vehicle. If he was lucky, no wildlife would pop up on the side of the road and make a last-minute dash across. There was no way he could make a sudden stop without risking flipping the vehicle.

The terrain was deserted, so he wasn't concerned with any unexpected traffic.

"Take the next left and we'll take the back roads to Crystal Lake."

J.T. slowed as much as he dared and skidded into the turn. Eve braced her feet against the dash.

Five minutes later they remained in the clear.

They'd lost them.

"You're certain there's no chance they can track us back to the cabin?"

"I'm certain. They were likely watching the Jamison place and hoping we would show up there."

Made sense.

J.T. couldn't deny the plausibility of her theory any longer. The situation damned sure appeared to be related to his work at the insurance agency.

He'd been gone from Gold Coast Life several

months. Strange that he was only learning now that there had been a problem.

J.T. HAD DECIDED EN ROUTE that he would contact Victoria as soon as they arrived back at the cabin. Eve would just have to deal with it. Victoria would be worried. His mother would be worried.

Maybe Eve had no one in her life to answer to, but that wasn't the case for him.

She unlocked the cabin's front door. "We need to make a list of as many of the high payouts made by your company over the past couple of years as you can recall." She went inside and tossed her bag onto the sofa. "We can interview the beneficiaries the way we did Mr. Jamison and see if there's a pattern of fraud."

J.T. closed the door behind him. He'd already come to that same conclusion. "There are eight that I specifically recall as being seven figures."

"You remember any of the names?" She ran her fingers through that gorgeous hair and started pacing. "We can track them down pretty quickly if the names aren't too common."

"The first thing we do is set some boundaries."

She stopped her pacing. "I thought we'd already done that."

"The company's client list is privileged information. I'll need to do that part on my own."

"You're kidding, right?" Her hands went to her hips, drawing his attention there.

He hated that he could recall every square inch of her toned body. Long legs, narrow hips, narrower waist and those breasts. Amazing.

"Are you listening to me?"

Whatever she'd said he'd missed entirely. "I'm sorry, what?"

She executed an about-face and started pacing again. "Those guys tried to kill me once already for interfering in their plan to—" she threw her arms up to show her frustration "—do whatever to you. So don't even pretend I'm not a part of this. I'm in this up to my eyeballs! There's no backing up now."

J.T. swallowed back the arguments, forcing the words that needed to be said to the tip of his tongue. "It would likely be in your best interest to proceed with your plans to leave. You've been paid for your services, right? There's no reason for you to stay."

Fury flashed in those blue eyes. "Wow. The way you put that, I could be a hooker."

He hadn't meant it that way. "I meant—"

"I know what you meant," she snarled. "Yes, I was paid by the man who hired me. Yes, I should be out of here by now. But I was trying to save your ass." Her eyes glittered with the mounting fury. "I have my reasons for seeing this through."

"And I appreciate that." He frowned. "I think. But this has nothing to do with you. I can take it from here. If I need backup, I have the Colby Agency."

"You are serious." She stamped toward him. "They know I double-crossed them. Now they'll want me, too. Not to mention that puts a serious black mark on my professional reputation."

Both were true. Damn it. He didn't want her… here. With him. She was too much of a distraction. The situation was only going to get more dangerous. The more he learned and the longer he evaded the enemy, the more desperate the enemy would become.

This was going to get ugly in a hurry.

She would be in jeopardy right alongside him, and that would put him in an awkward position.

"Frankly," he chose his words carefully, "your reputation is of little concern to me. However—" he held up a hand when she would have blasted him "—your actions have put you at risk, and that is a concern."

"Gee," she tossed back, "it's so comforting to know that my *actions*—which, by the way, were tailored to save your ass—are of a concern to you."

This was getting them nowhere. "I have to check in with the agency."

She shook her head firmly from side to side. "No way. We talked about that already."

"I trust the Colby Agency." He wasn't negotiating

this point. "In the unlikely event someone is monitoring the calls in and out of the agency, I'll use extreme caution in discussing our circumstances. But I am making the call."

She ripped her cell phone from her back pocket and thrust it at him. "Fine. Make the call."

As if that hadn't made her feelings on the matter perfectly clear, she stamped out of the cabin, swearing under her breath.

J.T. put a call in to Victoria's direct line. She would likely be at home, but the call would be transferred to her home phone or her cell. Victoria Colby-Camp was never out of touch to her staff.

When she answered, J.T. cut right to the chase. He gave her the condensed version. She was relieved to hear from him. There had been a few new developments in the situation with the abduction attempt of her granddaughter but nothing substantial.

As dangerous as his situation, the one with Jamie was terrifying. He knew Victoria's history. Having that kind of horror strike twice in one's life was too much for anyone to bear.

"J.T., Ian discovered unsettling evidence at your home."

Surprised by her words, he asked, "What kind of evidence?"

"A numbered account at a Cayman bank containing half a million dollars."

If she'd said they'd found a golden egg in his refrigerator, he wouldn't have been more surprised. "I don't have a clue what you're talking about." Half a mil? In an account with his name on it? Yeah, right. "Maybe I won a lottery I don't know about."

"I was certain that would be your response. It appears someone is laying out a carefully constructed setup with your name on it."

"At this point," J.T. admitted, "I would have said Arenas was setting me up to cover for his own crimes. But he's dead, so, it's definitely not him." He'd mulled over the other possibilities, but not one stood out for him. He'd worked with those people for years, respected every one of them. Including Arenas.

"Ian is attempting to trace the account's origin. We'll look into Arenas's death. And Paula Jamison's. Will that help?"

"Yes." Relief surged. "That would be very helpful. I don't have my cell, but you can reach me at this number." He rattled off the number.

"How is Eve?"

The question had him peering out the front window. She was leaning against her car, smoking a cigarette. He frowned. She didn't smoke.

What the hell did he know?

"She's…" How did he answer that question? "She's not the Eve I thought I knew."

"Are any of us really who others think we are?"

J.T.'s brow tugged into a frown. "This is more than that." He understood what Victoria was trying to say, but he couldn't swallow in such an easy pill what Eve had done to him.

"Think about it, J.T. We all show others what we want them to see. Our speech patterns—our entire behavior changes with each audience. Family, friends, colleagues…we have different personas for each situation. Isn't that a form of deception on some level?"

"Maybe." He braced his arm on the window frame and rubbed at the frown etched across his forehead. "I don't know what to think."

"Don't think," Victoria countered. "Not when it comes to affairs of the heart. The heart and the brain have very little in common. Trust your instincts the same way you did when you fell in love with Eve."

That wasn't the advice he'd wanted to hear. But coming from Victoria it merited contemplation.

He ended the call with a promise to keep her informed of his moves. Victoria had been like an aunt to him. She'd always been there for his family, particularly after his father had died.

He watched as Eve threw the cigarette down and glared at the cabin door.

Might as well put her out of her misery.

He walked to the door and opened it. Their gazes met. For an instant he couldn't move. He could only look into those eyes.

"Did you give her our location?"

J.T. shoved his hands into the pockets of his jeans and moved to the steps. He sat down on the top one. "No. She didn't ask. She trusts me."

Eve rolled her eyes.

"So, you smoke?" How many other things did he not know?

She shrugged. "Not for real. Once in a blue moon." She glared at him. "At moments like this when fools won't listen to me."

He braced his elbows on his knees. "I am a fool, that's for certain."

She strode over to him. "Let's just get this part over with, okay?" Feet wide apart, hands on hips, she stared hard at him. "I lied. Cheated. Did whatever I had to do to get close to you. I obtained the information I needed, and then I split. Get over it. Having your feelings hurt won't kill you." She hitched her thumb toward the road beyond the trees. "Those guys, they're not playing. They might want something out of you, but ultimately they want you dead."

He held up his hands. "I'm not arguing on any of those counts."

Suspicion narrowed her gaze. "What're you up to?"

He dropped his hands to his thighs. He briefed her on the latest findings by the Colby Agency. "Let's just get to the bottom of this so we can both get on with our lives."

"I've been there all along." She climbed the steps past him. "What took you so long?"

WHAT THEY NEEDED, Eve mused, was computer access and a different ride.

Computer access would be easy. The ride, maybe not so. She'd abandoned the rental at the movie theater. Her own car was a liability now.

"We need to borrow a vehicle," she announced as she gathered her bag and slung it across her shoulder.

"And I need my weapon," he countered.

They stood in the middle of the room staring at each other for ten or fifteen seconds.

"I suppose having you armed could prove useful."

His face lit up with sudden inspiration. "My bike." He nodded as the idea only he knew evidently gained momentum in his mind. "I have a street bike in my garage. We could use it."

Bike? "Are you talking about a motorcycle?" He didn't have a motorcycle. She'd been in his garage dozens of times.

He nodded. "Kawasaki. You might not have

noticed, since I had a special cover made for it. I rarely have a chance to ride it, but occasionally I take it for a spin."

"You have a 'crotch rocket' and you never mentioned it?" She hadn't been the only one keeping secrets. There were certain things people told each other when they decided to get married. Owning a racy motorcycle was definitely one of them.

"You smoke," he challenged, "once in a blue moon. Eve Mattson isn't even your name. I don't think owning a street bike is a big deal compared with the secrets you've kept. Besides, it wasn't really a secret. It just never came up. I was busy." He shrugged. "I didn't think about it."

Guys, they were all the same. The biggest sin known to humankind was always somewhat less of a transgression if they were the perpetrators. "Uh-huh."

She headed for the door, then stopped to face him. "Let's go spend some time at a computer café. Then we'll check out this bike of yours."

Admittedly, the prospect of climbing onto the back of a bike, him nestled between her spread thighs, held some major appeal.

But it would be yet another mistake.

And she'd already made one too many with him.

Chapter Ten

8:30 p.m.

J.T. parked Eve's newly damaged car one street over from his own. They cut between two houses and approached his home from the rear.

Crouched near the privacy fence, J.T. said, "I'll have a look around just to make sure no one's waiting for us to show up."

It wasn't completely dark yet, so getting close to the house without being seen wasn't going to be easy. He'd need to stay between the shrubs and the fence, keeping his head low or he'd be spotted by anyone choosing to look. She told him as much. He gave her an I'm-not-stupid look.

Eve reached into her bag and pulled out her Glock. "Here." She shoved it at him, butt first. "Take this. You might need it."

He looked from the weapon to her. "You sure about that?"

Maybe this was another mistake, but she wasn't about to send him in there unarmed. He'd already been ambushed once in his home. Besides, she felt reasonably certain he wasn't going to take off on his own. At this point he was fairly convinced that he was being set up or was in danger. She may not have seen the man who'd hired her, but she'd heard his voice as well as that of one of his colleagues.

J.T. needed her.

That realization made breathing difficult. "Yeah. Go."

He accepted the weapon. Dusk prevented her from labeling what she saw in his eyes. Relief maybe?

Staying beneath the level of the shrubs flanking his yard, he scrambled toward the rear entrance of the garage. Eve bit her lip, listened intently for any sound. The neighborhood was a quiet one. Most of the dog owners kept their pets inside at night. Few folks on this block had small children. The only sound was the traffic of the main cross street several blocks away. If a vehicle turned onto his street, she would hear it well before it reached his house—as long as she paid attention.

Eve adjusted the strap of her shoulder bag. Her stuff had gotten soaked the night before last, but the items that mattered—her weapon, binoculars and driver's license—were good to go. And, of course, the cell phone she would be lost without. She'd checked her e-mail via her cell earlier to see if anyone had contacted her regarding the J.T. situation. Nada. No calls, either. No question about where she stood with the enemy now.

What the hell was taking him so long? He was supposed to go in, get the bike and get out.

If she had to go in there and check on him…

A roar erupted in the quiet.

He'd started the bike. What the hell?

She braced to make a dash toward the house. The revving engine echoed louder. A blue-and-white blur sped past the gap between his house and the next. Her jaw dropped.

He'd left.

Left her.

Cursing, she pushed to her feet.

That was when she heard the tires squeal. She raced across the backyard, getting to the front corner of his house just in time to see the dark sedan barreling in the same direction in which his bike had disappeared.

They had been watching the house.

Damn it!

He'd left the garage's overhead-side door open. The automatic opener had been disengaged so that he could open it quietly by hand. Obviously he'd spotted the sedan on the street. Why the hell hadn't he come back out and told her?

He would go straight to his Colby Agency colleagues.

Ensuring one of two outcomes: his death or no way to track the person responsible for this mess. Considering what Victoria Colby-Camp had told him about the numbered account, he and maybe Arenas were supposed to be the scapegoats. If the person behind this setup determined that getting J.T. was no longer a viable scenario, he would simply disappear.

Then they would never know for sure who was behind this.

And J.T. could end up dead a month or a year from now. He'd spend the years to come looking over his shoulder.

Not acceptable.

Her fury building, she started to walk out of the garage but spotted what looked like a piece of paper on the windshield of his SUV. Something white anyway. Dusk had settled into near darkness. A few steps later and she had the note in her hand. She opened her cell phone for a light to read by.

Meet me at the place where we first had coffee.

If this was a setup to get her off his back by turning her over to the police…

Wait. He'd given her the benefit of the doubt when he had absolutely no reason to. She had to do the same for him. It was his handwriting.

She checked the door leading from the garage to the house. Locked.

She surveyed the SUV. Now, all she had to do was find his keys. He'd kept a spare set somewhere on the vehicle. She remembered him mentioning that he'd found a stellar hiding place. Not daring to turn on a light, she was left with no choice but to search by touch.

Not in any of the fender wells. She checked the front and rear bumpers. No such luck.

Oh well. She dropped to the floor and scooted her body beneath the vehicle. Using her cell once more for light, she scanned the chassis.

"Aha." The small metal box that contained an ignition key was a little dirty but readily identifiable. She pulled it loose, closed her phone and started to belly from under the vehicle.

The glow of headlights filled the garage.

Instinct sent Eve scooting to the far side of the SUV's underbelly.

In the driveway a car door slammed. The rasp of footsteps heightened her senses.

Adrenaline seared through her veins. She eased deeper beneath the SUV and froze, holding her breath.

The footsteps moved slowly along the drive. Inch

by inch. She turned her head in the direction of the open door. A wide stride cut through the stream of twin lights. Black leather lace-up shoes. Black trouser legs.

A lone male. He walked to the middle of the double-car garage and stopped. She didn't have to see to know that he was likely looking around for any clue as to where J.T. would have gone from here.

Then he started moving again.

Eve barely resisted the urge to attempt getting a look at the guy. But ending up dead wasn't on her immediate agenda.

The rustle of fabric told her he was digging in his trouser pocket. A few clicks of metal and the door leading into the house opened. Experienced at lock-picking. No mistaking which side of the law he was on. She recognized the traits. Most of her adult life had been spent on *that* side of the law.

She could make a run for it while he was inside, but J.T. had implied that she should bring his vehicle.

She could come back for the SUV.

Another reality throttled through her: The sedan had followed J.T. There had been plenty of time since she'd dragged J.T. out of here the night before last for anyone who wanted the opportunity to search the house to do so.

Why had this guy bothered going inside?

This wasn't about what was or wasn't inside the house—this guy was looking for her.

His associates had seen J.T. leave alone. They suspected she was here somewhere.

The urge to flee fired in her muscles.

Don't move.

Seconds turned into minutes. Sweat broke out on her forehead.

What the hell was he doing in there?

Was she making a mistake waiting him out?

If he had a gun, would he use it in a neighborhood setting like this?

It was dark outside now. That fact would be to his advantage, giving him cover, if he got her in his sights. The best strategy was to stay put, ride it out. Then he would think she'd been dropped off somewhere else or had moved on.

The measured footsteps echoing from inside warned of his impending exit from the house.

Once again Eve held her breath. As much as she'd like to get a look at this guy, she would like to get out of here alive a whole lot more. So she stayed perfectly still.

Just go, she urged silently.

Then he stopped…in the middle of the garage. His long legs sliced the beam of the headlights, highlighting his presence.

A man like him, a professional, would have well-honed instincts.

He sensed something was off…someone was close. He wasn't leaving until he was sure.

Her eyes widened as he turned and started toward the SUV.

Damn it. She'd given her Glock to J.T.

Where was the note, in her pocket?

Had she dropped it on the floor? If he noticed it, he would know she was here.

He stopped at the SUV's passenger-side door.

Her heart stumbled into an irregular pattern.

If he crouched down…

She wasn't waiting for his next move. She had to act. Now!

With one click she made the next move.

The SUV's alarm system kicked in—horn blowing, lights flashing.

The man backed up a step.

Stalled an instant.

Eve reacted to his hesitation.

Then he turned and walked briskly back to his car, dropped behind the wheel and shifted into Reverse.

The headlights grew distant and faded as he backed from the drive and, tires squealing, sped away.

Eve hit the button to stop the alarm, took a deep breath and exhaled some of the tension.

Get the hell out of here.

She slid from beneath the SUV, hit the unlock button and climbed inside. Without turning on the headlights, she backed from the garage and went in the opposite direction of the one the man had taken.

Taking a right at the first intersection, she rolled down the street where she'd left her car and her bag. Scanning the darkness, she hopped out, unlocked her car and retrieved her bag. She surveyed the street before climbing back into the SUV. No sign of a tail.

Now, if J.T.'s luck had held out, he would be waiting for her at the coffee shop off the West Loop. The one where they'd met to discuss taking care of the damages to his SUV.

She took a long, deep breath. This time it wasn't related to drawing in enough oxygen, but it was entirely connected to inhaling his scent. That spicy, musky, very male aroma that heated her blood, made her flesh tingle. It permeated the interior of his SUV. She sank more deeply into the luxurious leather seats.

God, she'd missed him.

Idiot.

How could she have fallen even a little for this guy? She knew better than to get emotionally involved with a job. J.T. was a job.

Still was.

Sort of.

Once this was over, she was out of here. She wasn't cut out for his whitewashed, white-collar lifestyle. Eve Mattson was not like J.T.'s colleagues at the Colby Agency. She wasn't even like J.T.

J.T. STOOD OUTSIDE THE coffee shop. He'd waited inside for the first ten minutes. But now, twenty minutes after his arrival, he was on the verge of driving back to his house to check on Eve.

She should have been here by now.

He'd tried the cell number he'd had for her, but that one was no longer in service.

He shouldn't have left her.

But he'd spotted two men and had made a snap decision.

Lead them away from her…. Lose them.

He rubbed his neck and refused to consider that she could have left again.

Left him.

It wasn't as if she hadn't warned him. He was very much aware that some sort of strategy was going down. A strategy that made him a scapegoat. She'd wanted him to know that.

There really was no reason for her to show up here. Her job was done.

She could get on with her life. Whatever and wherever that was.

Ten more minutes. He would wait ten more minutes, and then he would leave.

The longer he stayed in the open, the more likely he could be spotted. He needed a strategy of his own. At the top of his priority list was to determine who was behind what had apparently been a scam on the insurance company where he'd worked.

With Arenas dead, that opened up the possibility that someone else inside was involved. He'd made a list of more than half a dozen cases where the payout was seven figures or more. Until he was able to determine who was involved on the inside, he would try to measure how deeply and how far back the scam went.

Headlights down the street flickered. He stepped back into the alleyway between the coffee shop and the bookstore next door.

Black. SUV.

Relief flooded his chest.

His SUV.

Eve parallel-parked and climbed out.

As he watched her cross the street, that big old bag banging against her hips, something shifted in his chest. Deep in his chest.

When she reached the sidewalk, he called out to her. She diverted her course and headed for his shielded position.

"Someone came back to the house. A man. Alone."

Fear twisted his gut. "Are you all right?"

She looked taken aback that he'd asked. "I hid under your SUV."

"Did you get a look at him?"

A shake of her head. "Just his shoes."

"He was looking for you." More of that fear he hadn't wanted to label twisted in his gut.

"It would seem so."

He surveyed the street. "We should get out of here."

"I need coffee first."

A laugh burst from his chest. "Sure. Coffee sounds good."

They waited through the line. Got their favorite coffees and a snack, then found a booth in the darkest corner of the shop.

Her hair was mussed, but it looked good on her. A grin cut across his face.

She gave him a look. "What's that all about?"

"You have—" he reached out and swiped a smudge from her cheek "—a smudge."

She leaned away from his touch. "That happens when you crawl around under vehicles."

Yeah. He blinked, dropped his gaze and stared at the froth on his coffee. What was he doing? He didn't want to feel *this*. Didn't want to add insult to injury. She obviously hadn't felt the way he had. As she'd so eloquently put it, he had been a job.

And he'd been totally head over heels in love with a woman whose name he still didn't know.

That slowly simmering mix of anger and frustration ignited.

"We should go." He set his coffee aside.

She sipped long and deep. "Back to the cabin?"

He forced his mind to focus on business. "There's no reason to believe they know about the cabin. That may be the only place we're safe."

"I agree." She finished off her coffee. "You have a strategy in place?"

"Working on it." He slid out of the booth. He didn't want to be here anymore. Too many memories.

"You planning to share it with me?" She grabbed her bag.

"When we get to the cabin." He dug his keys from his pocket. "I'll go in first. You hang back until I give the all clear."

She laughed. "I can take care of myself. In case you hadn't noticed."

He didn't move as she walked away. Just stood there like the fool he was and watched her move.

Chapter Eleven

11:55 p.m.

"So." Eve leaned back in the leather chair and surveyed the list of names she'd written on the cabin's complimentary notepad. "We have Rebecca James, Damon Howe and Terrence Arenas. Arenas is dead. That leaves Howe and James. Would you lean more toward one of those names than the other?"

J.T. pushed off the sofa and started pacing. "Howe worked closest with Arenas. That puts him at the top of my list."

Eve circled the man's name. They'd gone over J.T.'s former colleagues and prioritized a list of who might be involved in this scam. He'd also organized a list of the big payout cases for the last two years he worked at Gold Coast Life. They'd narrowed down the addresses for each at the computer café. Only two names had multiple addresses. Tracking down the beneficiaries on that list wouldn't be difficult or terribly time-consuming. The sooner they got started, the closer they would get to finding the truth.

The goal was to determine if any of those people had had experiences similar to Paula Jamison's with collecting his or her death benefits. According to the insurance company's records, the payouts to the beneficiaries had been for the face value of the policies. If the beneficiaries had received less than that amount, someone had pocketed the remainder.

"I could talk to Rebecca James," J.T. said as he reclaimed his seat. "She and I were fairly close. Friends as well as colleagues. I still hear from her occasionally."

"Really?" Eve dropped the list and the pen on the table next to her chair. Her gaze narrowed on him before she could censor the reaction. "Friends, you say? Does that mean the random lunch kind of friends? Or maybe you had the occasional drink after work?"

He picked up on her too keen interest. "Both."

She tamped back the irrational reaction. "Good." She cleared her throat. "That should make getting information easier."

"Like—" he leaned forward, braced those muscular forearms on his knees and looked directly into her eyes "—an entry strategy."

She emulated his posture. "Exactly."

The stare down lasted several moments.

The anger he didn't want her to see was written all over his handsome face just as the tinge of jealousy she'd allowed to peek through had been thick in her tone moments ago.

Why were they doing this to each other?

Why couldn't she just walk away the way she'd always done before?

What the hell made this time—this man—different?

He schooled his expression. "I should check my voice mail. Since Victoria doesn't have your other cell-phone number, she would not've been able to reach me if the agency learned anything new about the Cayman account allegedly set up in my name."

Eve pulled her cell from her pocket and tossed it to him. "I need more caffeine." Eve got up and stalked to the kitchen. What she really needed was a stiff drink. But that wouldn't be smart. Considering her current inability to keep her thoughts and reactions conquered, the last thing she needed was her restraints loosened by alcohol.

Coffee would work for now.

When this was over, she was taking a couple of

weeks some place far away and discreet to exorcise this guy from her head.

Then she would get back on track with a new assignment and a new outlook.

She set the coffeemaker to brew and turned back to where J.T. sat listening to his voice mails. She'd worked with good-looking men before, some every bit as handsome as J.T. How the hell had she let him get to her on any level?

As if the thought had telegraphed itself to him, he turned toward her. The wild look in his eyes, the absolute fear on his face, made her heart contract prematurely.

Something was wrong.

He closed the phone, his hands shaking. "My mother is in the hospital."

Images of Ruth Baxley flashed in Eve's mind. Proud, strong woman. "What happened?"

He crossed to the counter and shoved the phone at her. "Someone broke into the house, questioned her regarding my whereabouts then ransacked the place."

A mixture of worry and anger exploded in her chest. "Is she okay? What's the damage?" What bastard would go after an old woman like that?

"Concussion." He snatched the keys to his SUV from where they'd landed near the sink. "A couple of cracked ribs." He swore. "Damn it! This is my fault.

I should have been protecting her. I should have seen this coming and put preventive measures in place."

"Don't be foolish, J.T. You had no idea they'd go after your mother." He was going to the hospital. Not good. Not safe.

He headed for the door. "I'll be back.…"

"Wait." Eve rounded the island that separated the kitchen from the living area. "This is what they want you to do. They'll be watching the hospital. There's no way to know what their next move is going to be. There are still too many unknowns to go in blindly. We have to act with caution."

If looks could kill, she would have dropped dead on the spot. "I don't give a damn about any of that. I'm all she's got." He glared at Eve. "She's all I've got. A whole army couldn't stop me from going."

"I'm coming with you." Eve dashed back to the coffeemaker and turned it off. She grabbed her bag and joined him at the door. "Someone needs to be watching your back." She had learned the hard way that distraction could get a person killed faster than most anything else.

For a blip in time he stared at her…just stared. She wanted to say something like *sorry* or *it'll be okay*. But the words couldn't get past that lump in her throat. He was worried and scared and…confused.

Because of her.

She shouldn't have cared.

Another mistake.

Mercy General, 1:00 a.m.

EVE BRACED FOR the elevator doors to open. She and J.T. had made it from the parking garage to the lobby without incident.

With tightened security measures she'd had no choice but to leave the Glock in the SUV. She felt defenseless, naked, without it.

The elevator bumped to a stop on the floor he'd selected. Eve held her breath as the doors glided open. She couldn't readily identify any of the men who'd given chase, but one or more would be here.

No question.

J.T. stepped out of the elevator, looked left first, then right, and then moved forward. Eve followed.

The long white corridor was quiet.

Hospitals and funeral homes were her least favorite places. The death of her parents had been intensely traumatizing to a seven-year-old child.

The door to Room 601 was protected by a man Eve recognized as one of J.T.'s Colby Agency associates. She couldn't recall his name—Peter or Patrick, something like that.

"O'Brien," J.T. said, acknowledging the man at the door.

Patrick O'Brien. Eve remembered now.

"She's resting," O'Brien said quietly. "You just missed Victoria. She'd been with her since she arrived at the E.R."

J.T. patted the other man's arm. "I appreciate your being here. And Victoria."

O'Brien nodded. His glance at Eve was fleeting. He didn't speak. She supposed everyone at the agency knew about her.

Why should she care?

As she followed J.T. into the room, she couldn't slough off the sting.

Whether she should or not, she did care.

Eve stayed near the door as J.T. went to his mother's bedside. The array of monitors beeped and hummed. A foreboding white bandage on the woman's forehead looked stark against her dark hair. The right side of her face was bruised and puffy.

Eve's throat constricted. This was her fault, too. She should never have taken this job.

Ruth Baxley had been nothing but kind to her…. And this was what she got for her trouble.

J.T. dragged the chair close to his mother's bed and settled in. His long fingers wrapped around her small hand. The misery that was sculpted into every line and angle of his face ripped at Eve's insides, made her want to kill whoever had done this.

She felt as if she should say something. Apologize. Pray. Something. But there was nothing she could say or do to make this right.

This was wrong on an elemental level that shook her to the core.

As the minutes turned into hours, she stood there, unable to move, and watched J.T. silently grieve this wrong. He hovered over his injured mother as if his mere presence would somehow heal her, make her comfortable at the very least.

At one point the poor woman opened her eyes. Her lips trembled into a smile. J.T. kissed her cheek, murmured softly to her. Fragile whimpers echoed across the room, screaming of the pain and the fear his mother suffered still. She'd lost her husband last year. The man who'd been her high-school sweetheart, who'd loved her for more than three decades.

Now she was alone except for her son.

And someone was trying to take him, too, away from her.

Eve tried to swallow and blinked at the sting in her eyes. The primal human emotions that played out before her were foreign to her. She had never had that kind of relationship with anyone. Not a single living soul.

Well, maybe when she was a little kid. She scarcely remembered those *normal* years.

Her mother and father had been killed in a car crash when she was seven. She recalled vividly standing in the cemetery at their graveside services. Snow had been a foot deep on the ground. She'd been so cold. And alone. A neighbor had held her hand. No siblings, no other family except for an aunt in Phoenix—a million miles away from Winnetka. The aunt hadn't bothered to fly in for the funeral. She did manage to show up at the airport in Phoenix when Eve arrived.

Everything had changed that day.

The heat of Arizona…the indifference of her crazy aunt.

Her childhood had ended that day in the cemetery.

Her aunt had declared that to earn her room and board, Eve would cook and clean. By the time Eve had turned ten, her aunt had been selling pictures of her to any pervert who'd cough up the cash. The Internet came next. Eve had been a star of more than one site by the time she was twelve years old.

Then she'd run away.

At thirteen she'd decided that living on the streets was better than living with her drunken aunt and her perverted friends.

Men had been a means to an end. Food, clothing or shelter. Nothing more. She'd learned how to con anything out of anyone without getting emotionally involved.

She hadn't been to school on a regular basis since she was eleven, so she'd taught herself. With all she knew, she could easily be a university graduate with a degree in foreign and domestic affairs.

But she didn't have a degree in anything but survival.

A nurse came in, jolting Eve out of her miserable musings.

She checked Ruth's vitals and conferred with J.T.

Eve stayed out of the way. Just watched and wondered what it would have been like to be loved that way.

5:35 a.m.

J.T. LOWERED HIS mother's hand to the bed and covered it with the sheet. She was sleeping again. He'd told her that he would need to leave soon but would be back. She'd been beside herself with worry for him. She'd kept saying that during the intrusion into her home and the beating that followed, all she could think about was whether J.T. was safe.

He would get those bastards. Whoever was responsible for this would pay dearly.

Eve still lingered around the door. She hadn't said a word since they'd come into the room.

Part of his anger and frustration included her. He

was so furious with her for allowing this to play out. He wanted to lash out. To shake the hell out of her for not telling him sooner so he could have headed all of this off before it escalated.

And at the same time he wanted to hold her. To keep her safe, too.

Who the hell was she that she could ram into his life, steal a big hunk of him and then turn out to be a stranger? Damn it.

He still didn't even know her name.

He kissed his mother once more on the cheek. Time to go.

He would find who was behind all of this, starting with Rebecca James.

He considered that plan of action for a moment. No, first he needed to track down some of the folks on the list. He needed to confirm the scenario he suspected. One client's story wasn't enough.

Then he would go to Rebecca and enlist her help in uncovering those behind this scam.

Eve's gaze shot to his as he turned and started for the door.

"Time to tackle that list."

Eve glanced at his mother and then back at him. "We'll need to take a back way out of here. They'll be watching."

He nodded. "I have a plan."

Outside the room, J.T. huddled with O'Brien. They shared one of those "man hugs." Eve hadn't realized the two were so close.

J.T. motioned for her to follow him. As they moved down the corridor, everyone they encountered became a suspect. Since visiting hours hadn't begun, only hospital personnel appeared to be on the floor. But Eve understood that uniforms and badges didn't mean the people they met weren't imposters.

Keeping a close eye on the corridor behind them, as well as each door they passed, she followed J.T. through the door marked *Linens*.

"Stay here." He took a look outside the door. "I'll be right back."

"Wait," Eve argued. "What're you—?"

Too late. He was out the door.

She paced the small room, working herself into a ball of frustration by the time he returned.

He closed the door behind him and started to strip off his clothes.

"What…?" Then she saw the scrubs in his hand. "I see." She nodded. "Good plan."

"I know." He dragged on the scrub pants with her watching like a naive schoolgirl. "O'Brien slipped his keys into my pocket. We'll take his car."

So that was what the hug was about. "Good

thinking." If he said *I know* again, she was going to deck him.

When he'd pulled on the scrub top, he gestured to a buggy full of soiled linens. "Climb in and cover yourself up."

She made a face. But then again, she'd been in worse places. Following his orders, she burrowed deep into the buggy and piled the dirty linens over her head. J.T. shoved his discarded clothes into the buggy with her. The enemy would be looking for the two of them—not a lone hospital employee.

The buggy bumped into motion. The going was smoother when they were in the corridor. She couldn't see a damned thing.

J.T. exchanged good mornings with those he passed in the corridor. Eve tried not to breathe too deeply. But if this ruse got them out of here, it would've been worth the stinky ride.

She felt the buggy's wheels bump over the elevator door guides. Though she wasn't privy to J.T.'s plan, she imagined he would take the elevator to the basement and attempt an exit from there.

The elevator stopped several times. The sound of people loading and unloading, chatting about the coming workday, lulled Eve. She was tired. No sleep was bad for one's reactions.

When the elevator bumped to a stop for the last time, she felt the buggy move out the open doors.

"Wait until I give you the word," J.T. murmured.

More bumping and rolling. Finally the buggy stopped.

"Give me a minute." He reached into the buggy for his clothes.

Now he was being modest?

He tapped the buggy. "Come on."

She unburied herself and stood. He offered his hand while she climbed out. Eve righted her clothes and smoothed her hair.

"What now?"

"There's a maintenance exit over there." He indicated the west end of the basement. "O'Brien's car is parked in the E.R. visitor's lot."

That meant a walk around the building.

At this hour they would no longer have the cover of darkness. Speed and caution would be necessary.

J.T. hesitated at the exit. "If we run into trouble, take cover and call 9-1-1. I'll try and keep them distracted."

Eve gawked at him. "Why don't you take cover and call 9-1-1? I can keep them distracted as well as you can."

"Are we really going to argue about this?"

The determination on his face told her he wasn't

budging. "Whatever." She would call 9-1-1 all right, but then she would do what needed to be done.

Once outside, they weaved carefully between cars, moving toward the other end of the property.

J.T. stopped next to a minivan. He nodded in the direction of his SUV. To the right, a couple spaces over and behind the SUV, a dark sedan had parked. Two men waited inside. The sedan had been backed into the spot for a quick exit.

"I can't get the Glock." Eve needed her weapon. J.T. couldn't exactly go back to his house for his.

"We'll come back for it."

Yeah, yeah. But what about the meantime?

Keeping low, they made their way to the E.R. end of the building. They weren't likely to be spotted leaving from a good distance from where the SUV was parked.

In O'Brien's car, she turned to J.T. "Where to first?"

"I thought we'd go down the list, see if we can confirm a pattern."

"Before going to see your *friend* Rebecca?"

She cringed when his expression reflected the idea that he'd once again picked up on her dislike of the concept that he had a friend named Rebecca.

Amazingly dumb.

Eve scooted low in the seat as they exited the E.R. parking area, just in case any attention was directed at all departing vehicles. They would expect two passengers. She needed them to see only one.

When J.T. gave the all-clear sign, she scooted back into the seat and tugged on her seat belt.

"Sorry about your mom." She meant that. She also needed to shift the subject away from Rebecca what's-her-name.

"Me, too."

They drove in silence for a minute or so.

"I've been thinking," J.T. said abruptly.

She shifted her attention to his profile. "And?"

"There's no reason for your continued involvement in this situation. I can drop you off…."

That he didn't look at her told her this was the it's-over-get-lost moment.

"What about backup?" She hated that her voice sounded a little thin.

"The Colby Agency will back me up." Still he refused to look at her.

Determination hardened inside her. "No way, Baxley. I'm in on this until the end."

"There's no need—"

"Forget it," she argued. Then to end it once and for all, she added, "I have a vested interest in the outcome. So don't even think about trying to blow me off."

He did look at her then. One glaring moment. "What kind of interest?"

"That's none of your business." She folded her arms over her chest and stared straight ahead. "But it's to my benefit to stay."

He made a scoffing sound. "I should have known you hadn't hung around this long for any other reason."

"That's right," she lied.

Let him think what he would.

She wasn't going anywhere until this was done.

Chapter Twelve

Chicago, 7:15 a.m.

Victoria was running late this Monday morning. She placed her coffee mug in the sink. Two cups and she still didn't feel completely awake. Food had held no appeal whatsoever to her.

After last night's scare with Ruth, J.T.'s mother, and a long stay at the hospital, Victoria had reluctantly informed Ian that she wouldn't arrive at the office until closer to nine.

Merri Walters had arrived at seven to relieve Jane Sutton. Jamie had perked up immediately when Merri peeked into her room. The child truly adored the newest member of the agency's staff. Victoria felt immensely comfortable with Merri on duty.

Since she'd only arrived in Chicago two weeks ago, she was one of Victoria's first choices for keeping watch over Jamie. As strange as it sounded, the logic was sound. The young woman had lived in Nashville her entire life. As a brand-new transplant to this city, Merri represented the least possible threat of having been pinpointed by the enemy.

Victoria despised that feeling of uncertainty. She trusted every member of her staff without reservation, however, when the enemy was seeking ways to infiltrate the agency, the regular faces were the easiest targets. Daily routines could be observed over a period of time, allowing for the discovery of opportunity.

Opportunity was all the enemy needed.

Merri had no daily routine. She was too new to the city and the agency. Until three days ago her name and face wouldn't have even been associated with the agency at all. That provided a sense of added security for Victoria where her granddaughter's safety was concerned.

She yearned for this to be over. But her staff was doing everything possible. This, too, would simply take time. As well as persistence. Even a lucky break or two wouldn't hurt.

Victoria's desperation was showing.

Last night's hours at the hospital had reminded Victoria all too well of how fragile life could be. Seeing Ruth lying there so helpless had shaken Victoria. She'd checked with Patrick O'Brien first thing this morning. Ruth was doing well, particularly after her son's visit last night.

According to Patrick, J.T. had been accompanied by Eve. Victoria's romantic side couldn't help hoping the two would end up together. No matter what Simon and Ian had learned about Eve, Victoria had noted the way the young woman had looked at J.T. Victoria knew true love when she saw it in another woman's eyes.

Despite having met Eve Mattson on only three or four occasions and always in a social setting, Victoria was certain of her assessment. There were times, unfortunately, when love wasn't quite enough. At times one had to overcome great personal obstacles in order to follow one's heart.

Victoria hoped Eve would have the courage and strength to overcome hers. J.T. deserved to end up with the woman he loved.

When Victoria had spoken to Ian, he'd updated her on the alleged Cayman account in J.T.'s name. A dummy corporation had set up the account. The agency's research department was attempting to track down the sources behind the corporation. That could take weeks or perhaps even months. Corporations of that sort were often designed to avoid taxes. The more difficult they were to track down, the better for those involved who wanted to keep certain assets hidden.

Victoria knew with complete certainty that J.T. wasn't the source of the corporation or the account. But finding out who was could very well help with whatever was happening to him now.

But it would take precious time.

"Victoria."

Victoria turned as Merri entered the kitchen. "Yes." Victoria ensured that she maintained eye contact when she spoke to Merri. Having lost her hearing in her twenties, Merri relied almost solely on lipreading. She was trained in signing but preferred the less intrusive method of lipreading. Her preference was understandable, given the few years she'd been deaf.

"Jamie wanted me to hold this bear for her." Merri offered the stuffed animal to Victoria. "I was admiring it, and I noticed something you need to be aware of."

Victoria accepted Mr. Bear. It was Jamie's favorite toy. She never went anywhere, including bed, without the cuddly animal.

"It's the eyes." Merri gestured to the stuffed animal. "The diamondlike centers are not right. They've been added."

Victoria's pulse jumped as she stared at the face of the stuffed animal. Lucas had given the toy to Jamie on her first Christmas. It had been at her side ever since. Many trips back to the mall or supermarkets had been required to find a lost Mr. Bear.

She studied the eyes closely. Merri was right. The center of the eyes were like small diamonds. Had they always been that way? Victoria wasn't sure. She'd never noticed. She lifted her gaze to Merri. "Perhaps the eyes have always been this way." She would certainly have Ian check it out while Jamie was in school. That was the one place the bear didn't go—a decision not easily reached or enforced.

Merri shook her head, seeming confused or frustrated. "I've seen this before."

Victoria frowned. She was the one who didn't understand. "What do you mean?"

"My first assignment with Nashville's Metro Division," Merri explained. "I worked undercover as a nanny for a mob boss. His daughter had a bear similar to this one. The original eyes had been augmented with these. Those diamondlike stones are tracking chips."

More of that pulse-throbbing adrenaline raced through Victoria's veins. "Are you sure? You didn't notice before?" Victoria was grasping at straws. How could this have happened?

Merri shook her head. "This morning is the first time Jamie allowed me to hold Mr. Bear. She asked me to take care of him while she goes to school."

Victoria moved to the counter where she'd left her cell phone. "I'm calling Ian."

"Excuse me?"

Victoria shook her head and reminded herself not to turn away or look down when she spoke. "I'm sorry. I said I'm going to call Ian. If this is what you believe it is, we need to know when and how the change occurred."

Merri nodded. "Many parents do this in case their child is abducted."

Victoria was aware such technology existed, but Jim and his wife, Tasha, hadn't mentioned taking any of those precautions. "I need to find out," she said to Merri.

"There will be a serial code on the backs. Difficult to see but there," Merri explained. "That number can be traced back to the original purchaser. If your son or daughter-in-law made the purchase, you can confirm that quite easily."

Victoria's fingers stumbled on the numbers. Fear had tightened like a noose around her neck. As the call went through with an initial ring, she reached out, putting her hand on Merri's arm. "Thank you. This could make all the difference."

Dear God, Victoria wished Jim or Lucas were here.

Chapter Thirteen

1:15 p.m.

J.T. spread the small notepad pages on the table and stared at his handwritten results.

There was no question. Someone high enough up the food chain at GCL had embezzled millions of dollars. Six payments over two years. The other two he'd considered had been paid in full.

The six were simply the ones he'd found during this rudimentary investigation.

There could be others. Many others.

"If the difference in payments went into that account with your name on it," Eve offered, "you could have a hell of a time proving your innocence."

All too true. "Victoria indicated there was around half a million in the account." He gestured to the pages. "That could potentially be a hell of a lot more than half a million."

"There could have been additional moves. With-drawals." Eve shook her head. "Someone set you up but good."

"Every one of these client payouts were approved by Arenas." That part stuck in J.T.'s gut. He had known the man well.

He'd thought he'd known Eve well, too.

"A dead man who can't defend himself." Eve sipped her iced coffee. "Kind of convenient, if you ask me."

"Damned convenient." J.T. glanced at the clock on the wall over the coffee shop's serving counter. Almost one-thirty. "We should head for the restaurant soon."

Eve followed his gaze and noted the time herself. "You're sure she'll show up?"

"She'll show up." He gathered the pages and folded the stack before tucking them into the pocket of his jeans. A change of clothes and a shower would have been nice, but there hadn't been time.

Since leaving the hospital, they had been covering ground as quickly as possible to reach all the names on the list. Only two of the eight names on his list had received the full death benefit specified by their policies. The others had been strong-armed, in a manner of speaking, into taking significantly less than the policy's face value.

It appeared someone had stolen millions.

Terror tactics. This could be called nothing else. The beneficiaries had been threatened, terrorized to a degree, to accept far less than had been contractually promised.

J.T. intended not only to clear himself but also to see that this travesty was set to rights. He thought of Leonard Jamison, physically disabled and living alone with no means to hire help of any sort. He'd seen much of the same with the other clients.

Clients seemed to be chosen based on rigid criteria. Few or no remaining family members, meager financial resources—like Paula Jamison. As long as her husband had been living, her personal finances were great—because he had a high-paying job. But after his death the insurance policy had been her only hope for financial security without his income. Another criterion appeared to be the selection of those who knew little about the way insurance worked and who did not possess the means to have the matter investigated. They simply accepted the paltry payments offered.

One of the beneficiaries, Helen Talley, for example, had depended wholly on her husband for taking care of business matters. She knew nothing of how such things worked. She had been the quintessential victim.

J.T. hesitated before leaving the table. He set his attention on Eve. "Is Eve your real name?" He had asked that question before. She'd hedged.

When she didn't answer right away, he added, "Give me something here. I can't keep pretending it doesn't matter. We're working together. Striving for the same goal."

"Yes," she said, her expression blank. "Satisfied?"

"Mattson? Or is it one of many others you've used?"

She looked away. "Mattson is the name of an actress I used to idolize. I wanted to be her."

The pain in her voice tugged at him. Made him want to know more. But he couldn't push her any harder than that. He wanted to kick himself for caring. For even wondering about her past.

Couldn't be helped. His feelings wouldn't be turned off that easily.

"Thank you."

She looked at him then.

She didn't respond, not verbally anyway. But he saw the uncertainty, the confusion in her eyes.

Enough for now.

Outside the coffee shop, Eve surveyed the street, as did he. So far there had been no sign of a tail. They'd succeeded in escaping the hospital without drawing attention, and that had set the precedent for the day so far.

It was almost eerie.

J.T. settled behind the wheel of O'Brien's car. If the bad guys understood that he was onto what they'd been up to, wouldn't they expect him to call on the clients involved?

Yet no one had been waiting for him to show. Each visit had gone off without a hitch.

They either had another strategy in place or were some really stupid bad guys.

Judging by how much money they had stolen over the past couple of years, he was relatively certain they were not stupid.

There was something else in the works.

"This Rebecca," Eve ventured, "is trustworthy?"

"To my knowledge." J.T. eased out of the parking spot and headed for the Magnificent Mile. "I've never had any reason to believe otherwise."

"Is that your usual standard of measure?"

Irritation kicked him in the solar plexus. "Until recently, yes."

Her silence let him know his words had hit the mark he'd intended.

Part of him wanted to demand why she didn't just go. She'd said she had something to gain, but he didn't see how that was possible.

Unless…she was the fail-safe individual. The one who ensured he was never too far out of reach, that he took all the steps that would ultimately do him no good except for putting his mark on each piece of evidence.

His first instinct was to give her the benefit of the doubt. But as she'd pointed out, maybe that wasn't such a good measure.

But it was one he'd lived by his whole life. He'd learned from the two people he trusted most—his parents. He wondered where Eve had learned her values.

Did it really matter?

She was a stranger to him. He had no legitimate reason to wonder anything about her. When this was done she would disappear again and he'd have to start the grieving process all over.

That was what he'd been doing for the last two weeks or so…grieving.

Because he'd stupidly trusted her, trusted his heart.

Gloom settled deep in his soul as he drove the few miles to their destination. Her continued silence only added another layer of dejection.

The worst part was he shouldn't have cared.

"There's a parking garage," she pointed out, hauling him out of the troubling thoughts.

He made the turn into the garage and found an empty space. Street parking was virtually impossible to snag on the famous street.

"What if this is a setup?" Eve shoved her door

closed and met him at the rear of the vehicle. "She could be the one instead of Arenas. I'm finding it seriously weird that no one lay in wait at any of the addresses we visited this morning."

"I guess we'll find out." J.T. kept his eyes and ears open as he moved out of the dimly lit garage onto the sidewalk.

The Mag Mile hosted the usual summer crowd of tourists window-shopping and workers rushing back to the office after a late lunch. Getting lost in the crowd was easy enough. The popular restaurant Rebecca had chosen would provide anonymity, as well. Quiet and deserted were never the best options for blending in.

J.T. gave Rebecca's name to the hostess, who immediately led them through the waiting crowd to a corner table, which offered as much privacy as could be expected in a high-profile tourist hotspot. Rebecca had already ordered her usual glass of white wine. She looked up and smiled as they approached.

"J.T." Rebecca stood and gave him a hug.

"It's good to see you, Becca."

"And who's this?" Rebecca asked as her attention shifted to Eve.

HAD THE WOMAN really just asked that? Eve resisted the urge to roll her eyes. *And who's this?* Like Eve was a child or a pet.

"This is my friend Eve Mattson."

His *friend?*

The other woman had extended her hand, while Eve was still reeling at the idea that Rebecca James didn't know who she was. She and J.T. had been engaged for a month, were supposed to get married two weeks ago—and one of his *friends* didn't know who Eve was?

There was something wrong with that picture.

Had they not lunched or had drinks in the past two months?

Eve gave the extended hand a brisk shake but she didn't bother with the nice-to-meet-you line. Lying had never been a problem for her, but why bother? She couldn't care less what sort of impression she made on this woman.

Rebecca was the kind of woman other women loved to hate: beautiful, stick thin but with a great bust and long legs. She dressed like a politician's wife, discreet, sophisticated. *How nice.*

When they'd settled at the table, J.T. pulled out his pages of notes. "This is what I've come up with so far."

Rebecca scooted closer to him. "Well, let's have a look." She leaned even closer to see the pages.

Eve wasn't buying it for a minute. She could see the notes clear across the table.

"I picked the eight largest payouts over the past

two years," J.T. explained to the attentive woman. "Six of the beneficiaries received significantly less than the policy's value. The tactics for achieving the lower payouts were clearly criminal."

Rebecca pursed her demurely painted lips a moment. "I recognize these names." She looked at J.T. then. "These are payouts Terrence cleared. In fact, several are clients he brought to the company."

"He did clear the payouts," J.T. confirmed. "I didn't know he'd brought any of the clients in."

"Definitely. In the early days, before his promotion. He was quite the salesman."

Eve had a feeling old Rebecca was a pretty good saleswoman herself.

"Can you confirm the payments claimed by the beneficiaries?"

"Of course." Rebecca moved her head from side to side, her expression somber. "This does not look good." She heaved a sigh. "I'm beginning to suspect Terrence may have committed suicide, after all."

"The preliminary exam indicated foul play," Eve countered, snapping out of her hatefest long enough to take a jab at showing her up.

"That's right," the other woman agreed. "But I spoke with Terrence's attorney yesterday, and he indicated that the police are leaning toward suicide." She looked from Eve to J.T. "I don't know if you've heard, but he hanged himself—or appears to have done so. There were signs of a struggle, and that's the reason for the other suspicions. There's nothing official yet."

"Becca, is there any way to get into Terrence's files? I don't want to accuse a man I not only trusted and respected but also who isn't here to defend himself."

If he called her Becca one more time, Eve was pretty sure she would throw up.

"Since he retired a few months ago," Rebecca began, "his internal files were absorbed by various colleagues. We can look, but I doubt there's anything to find. If your suspicions are accurate, I'm certain he would have covered his tracks."

"If your suicide theory is correct," J.T. commented, "he may have sensed he was about to be caught." He glanced at Eve. "He apparently had reservations about any evidence he left behind."

"What about that guy Damon Howe?" Eve put in. "You said he worked closely with Terrence."

"Is it possible Howe could have been involved with Terrence?" J.T. asked.

"You didn't hear?"

Eve tensed. Judging by the grim tone of the other woman, the news wasn't good.

"Hear?" J.T. prompted.

"He has cancer. He moved to Mexico to pursue a new kind of treatment. The last time I spoke to his wife, she said that his condition had deteriorated. He doesn't have long."

"By default, that leaves you," Eve suggested.

J.T. shot her a look.

Rebecca James blinked. "I suppose it does." She managed a halfhearted smile for J.T. "I guess the two of us are the prime suspects in a case the authorities aren't even aware of."

That she hung on to J.T.'s gaze with her own should have ticked Eve off all the more, but her instincts had started to hum.

That was the goal, she realized: to eliminate anyone involved in the fraud before the authorities were in the loop. That way any one of a number of folks could be deemed the scapegoats.

The perfect crime. Set up your closest colleagues, then kill them off one at a time.

Except for Howe, of course. And nature was taking care of that loose end.

When things got dicey, the bad guy—or woman—simply pointed at the evidence.

Brilliant.

Eve gave herself a mental shake and again zeroed in on the conversation.

"I think that's the route to go before this gets completely out of control," Rebecca was saying.

What was the suggested course of action?

"The caretaker will let you into the house?" J.T. asked.

Eve's attention swung back to Rebecca. What the hell had she missed?

"Absolutely. I was friends with Terrence for many years. I'll tell Carlton that I'm looking for a file Terrence may have brought home from work. He won't question me."

Eve's instincts were screaming at her now. "If you were such good friends with Arenas," she pressed, "didn't you suspect what he was doing?"

Rebecca looked taken aback. "There was never any reason to suspect him of wrongdoing. Terrence was an outstanding claims auditor. His reputation was stellar. His personal finances always seemed in perfect order. I can't imagine why he would do this."

"For millions of dollars," Eve offered. Was the woman dense?

"Remember," J.T. emphasized, "I considered Terrence my friend, as well."

Eve resisted the impulse to tell J.T. that his words carried no impact. He'd trusted her.

The reality of that statement pricked her with guilt.

The waiter arrived with the drinks Rebecca had taken the liberty of ordering. White wine all the way around. Eve hated white wine, but she didn't let that stop her from having a big gulp. She needed something to wash down all this garbage. This woman was up to something. Maybe J.T. couldn't see it, but Eve saw right through her too-sweet facade.

When they'd placed their lunch orders, J.T. added, "I don't think either of us is accusing Terrence of illegal activity at this point." He said this more to Eve than to Rebecca.

Eve shrugged. "He's dead. I doubt he cares."

J.T. shot her another of those looks. "However, he may have had evidence against whoever was responsible."

"That may very well be why he's dead," Rebecca suggested.

Eve swallowed more of her wine. If she survived this meal without barfing, it would be a miracle.

J.T. really was far too trusting.

But she sensed that he was about to learn a very valuable lesson.

"So," Rebecca said when the waiter had moved away, "what do you do, Eve?"

Eve smiled at the pretty woman. "Me?" She tucked the linen napkin into her lap. "I'm a problem solver."

J.T. was glaring at her. She didn't have to look to know; she could just feel those dark eyes boring into her.

"A problem solver?" Rebecca made a humming sound. "Interesting. Do you work here in the city?"

"The world is my office." Eve decided to give her something to think about. "I travel a lot. Analyze situations and determine the most efficient route to solve the problem."

The woman held her gaze as she sipped her elegant white wine. Everything about her was ultrachic and conservative. Perfect—down to her French manicure.

"How did you and J.T. meet?" she inquired.

"Actually," J.T. cut in, "she rear-ended my SUV."

Rebecca's eyes widened. "Really?"

"Afterward," Eve chimed in, "we went back to his place and had hot, sweaty negotiation sex."

Rebecca choked on a swallow of her fancy wine, which to Eve tasted like bad beer.

J.T.'s sour look had turned to a flat-out glower.

"He's quite good," Eve provided, "in case you didn't know."

J.T. cleared his throat and shuffled his note pages together.

"Actually," Rebecca said with a sly look at Eve, "I do know."

Conversation was a little stilted after that. J.T. rambled on about work at the agency. Rebecca waxed on about how things had changed in the months since he'd left Gold Coast Life. Eve worked at keeping her eyes from rolling back in her head far enough to see the roots of her hair.

Mainly she spent the time banishing images of classy, uptight Rebecca rolling in the sheets with J.T. The two would be perfect together. Both smart and beautiful and sexy.

Funny, Eve never once had this problem before. Not once.

The men she encountered were typically associated with her work. And work, well, it was work. She never got emotionally involved or personally attached. In. Get the goods. Out.

Uncomplicated.

What the hell had happened this time?

Her gaze settled on the man on the other side of the table.

He'd taken something from her, something she couldn't seem to move on without.

That dark gaze collided with hers as if he'd sensed her watching him.

Beyond the frustration and defensiveness she saw the answer….

He had loved her like no one else ever had.

Like no one else ever would.

The intensity of his feelings had stolen her edge. She was lost without it…without him.

Eve looked away.

He could never know.

She was wrong for him.

He deserved better.

He deserved something real…. This wasn't real.

She wasn't real.

Chapter Fourteen

5:30 p.m.

"She's not here." Eve pointed out the obvious.

J.T. gritted his teeth. He needed to focus on this investigation. Saying to her what he wanted to say at the moment would be a waste of time and energy. Not to mention the resulting blow up that would distract them from what they were here to do.

"She'll be here," he stated firmly. "She had a meeting. It may have run longer than expected. Happens all the time."

"A meeting. Yeah."

Enough. "What's your problem?" He shifted in the seat of his borrowed car to glare at her. "You don't even know Rebecca. You have absolutely no reason to believe she's involved in this any more than I am. Why the bullying?"

Eve made an unpleasant sound. "Just because you're blind doesn't mean I am. She's playing you like a well-tuned guitar. You just don't see it."

Damn. He shifted his attention to the house across the street. He wasn't doing this. Whatever Eve's problem, she could think what she wanted.

The only real evidence they had at the moment that pointed to anyone in particular was Leonard Jamison's word that it was Arenas.

The clients were all associated with him somehow, but that wasn't evidence.

They needed a connection to the numbered account in the Caymans. And right now that connection was J.T. himself. But he hadn't set up the account, hadn't transferred any money into it.

What bothered him more than anything was the way this whole thing had come out of nowhere. He'd worked at the insurance agency for four years. Not once had he suspected a single one of his colleagues of anything less than honorable conduct.

How could he have been that blind?

The woman in the passenger seat plopped her head back against the headrest and blew out a disgusted breath.

Maybe the same way he'd been blind to her true agenda.

How could he continue working for the Colby

Agency when he obviously didn't have the necessary insight into people?

A long talk with Victoria was in order when this was over.

He was sitting here, completely in the dark, so to speak, while his mother was in the hospital for reasons he hadn't seen coming.

Turning this investigation over to the agency would likely be best for all involved.

Then Eve could move on with a clean conscience.

He wasn't buying that whole hanging around for some added payoff. She just didn't want him to know she was worried about him.

Funny, from what he'd seen so far, she wasn't the type to worry.

Or to hang around once she was finished.

Just stop thinking, J.T.

He closed his eyes and exiled the confusion.

For the next ten minutes he managed to do exactly that. His attention remained focused on the house as he replayed all that he knew about the defrauded clients and the man he'd considered a friend. He hated to hear about Damon Howe. Could he be the one who'd taken the money? Medical bills were likely mounting. Unorthodox treatments could be costly.

"This is ridiculous," Eve complained, finally breaking the awkward silence.

"Give me your cell." He held out his hand. She dropped the phone in his palm without touching him. He entered Rebecca's number and waited through the four rings that activated her voice mail.

He closed the phone and handed it back to Eve. "She's obviously still in the meeting."

Eve shoved the phone into her pocket. "I don't know about you, but I'm sick of waiting." She opened her door. "I'm going in."

"Eve!"

She was halfway across the street before he was out of the car. "Eve! Damn it! You can't go in there."

It was an outright miracle that the caretaker hadn't noticed them loitering in the street already. In this neighborhood people called the police when strangers loitered for too long.

Eve didn't slow. She marched right up the walk. He caught up with her at the steps.

"You can't—" he snagged her arm, pulled her around to face him "—go in there like this. We have to wait for Rebecca."

"Brace yourself, Baxley. Your *friend* isn't coming."

Eve jerked free of his hold and double-timed it up the steps.

J.T. followed.

"Eve, wait." He was tired, frustrated and plain sick of this whole situation.

At the door she turned to face him. "It's not a big deal, J.T. We'll knock. Mr. Whatever His Name will come to the door, and we'll tell him we're meeting Rebecca here. He'll ask us in, and we'll snoop around when he isn't looking."

J.T. shook his head. "We're not knocking. We're not going in."

The sound of a car approaching drew his attention to the street. Not Rebecca. Damn. She knew how important this was. What was the hold up? He could buy the prolonged meeting excuse for only so long.

When he turned around, Eve was no longer standing next to him. The door yawned wide-open.

He swore.

For a second he considered just getting back into the car and driving away. This had gotten completely out of control. But the thought of his mother lying injured in that hospital bed reminded him that this wasn't just about him.

He walked through the open door. "Eve." He surveyed the massive foyer.

When he got his hands on her, he was going to—

"J.T.!"

"Where are you?"

"Kitchen."

He wandered past the enormous great room and formal dining room. He'd attended a couple of parties here, but the front living area was as far as he'd ever gotten.

The kitchen sprawled across a major portion of the back of the house. Eve stood in the middle of the room.

A man lay on the floor at her feet, blood pooled around his body.

As J.T. slowly approached, Eve glanced at him. "Carlton, I presume."

J.T. had never been a police officer or a detective in a crime unit, but certain things he knew from his training at the Colby Agency.

"Don't touch anything," he warned.

"No kidding," she snapped. "I know my way around a crime scene, Baxley."

J.T. refused to ask. The more he learned about the woman, the more he realized he didn't know her.

It was scary.

He knelt next to the man, careful not to disturb the positioning of his body or the puddle of blood. He checked the carotid artery. No pulse. His skin was cold, his lips a pale blue.

J.T. lifted his hand. Rigor mortis had begun.

"He's been dead for a while."

J.T. looked up at Eve. "Yeah." He pushed to his feet and backed away from the corpse. "Call 9-1-1."

"Don't be ridiculous. Your friend is supposedly on her way. She can call." Eve headed across the room.

"Meanwhile, we'll be taking advantage of the situation to see what we can find."

"Eve," J.T. growled, "we're not touching anything and we're calling 9-1-1."

When he would have stalked after her, something on the floor caught his eye. He moved closer and crouched to get a better look. A handgun. Black. Halfway under the refrigerator. Taking a quarter from his pocket, he eased the weapon from under the fridge and leaned down, studying it more closely.

Glock.

"Eve!"

No answer.

He pushed to his feet and went in search of her. She could be into anything. God only knew what she would do if he didn't keep an eye on her.

Down a second hall that led deep into the east end of the house, he found her. In a home office or study. She sat behind the desk, her fingers flying over the computer keys.

"Terrence's computer has been wiped."

"Are you certain?" J.T. moved up next to her, leaning down to view the screen when he'd intended to tell her to get away from the desk.

"Nothing but the original software on here."

"What about CDs? External hard drives? Any sort of storage device."

"I've checked all the drawers." She pushed out of the chair. "The whole room has been cleaned out."

"But his body was found only a few days ago."

"He lived alone?" Eve asked as she walked around the room, looking on empty shelves and behind the window curtains.

J.T. shrugged. "He was a widower. He lived alone as far as I know."

She turned around. "You friend's not here yet, is she?"

J.T. shook his head. "We really need to call the police." He moistened his lips. "But first, there's something you need to see."

She followed him back into the kitchen. He pointed to the Glock on the floor. "Is that your weapon?"

Before he could stop her, she reached down and picked it up, looked it over. "It's mine."

Their gazes locked in a silent knowledge.

Tension throbbed between them for four, then five, beats.

"You realize there's only one way it got here," she said, her voice low, stiff.

"Yes." The weapon had been in his SUV at the hospital.

"You also realize that only one person knew we were coming here."

He nodded slowly. "Yeah."

EVE TURNED ALL THE WAY around in the kitchen.

No sirens.

No police.

No bad guys.

No Rebecca.

They had arrived well before the designated time. It was thirty or thirty-five minutes past that time now.

She drew in a really deep breath. The smell became more prominent. *Gas.* Her gaze fastened onto J.T.'s once more.

The Glock slipped from her fingers and clattered on the floor.

The words tumbled out of their mouths simultaneously.

"We need to get out of the house."

Eve lunged toward the French doors on the other side of the room.

J.T. beat her there and wrenched the handle downward.

Locked.

Damn!

His fingers fumbled on the locks.

"Hurry!" she urged.

He yanked the door open.

She pushed him through the opening.

He almost lost his balance but didn't lose his forward momentum.

He twisted his body and rushed back toward her.

"Run!" she screamed at him. What the hell was he doing?

Eve dove out the door.

He grabbed her hand.

Her whole world seemed to lapse into slow motion.

Her legs wouldn't move fast enough.

He was pulling her.

Not fast enough.

The boom blasted in her ears a split second before the ground shook beneath her feet.

The ground rushed up to meet her.

Eve grunted with the impact.

A few seconds passed before she could move.

Move!

She scrambled to her feet.

Where was J.T.?

He was getting to his feet right behind her. He staggered.

"You okay?" She shook her head, hadn't heard her own words. Her ears felt stuffed with cotton.

He looked her over, then turned back to the house. Fire had engulfed the middle section of the enormous house. The kitchen. The explosion had been focused in the kitchen—right where she and J.T. had been busy assessing the body.

The enemy had known that they would linger where the body had been left.

The police would come after the explosion and find them injured or dead, at the very least, looking even more guilty of more than one crime.

Whatever was left of her weapon was in there…. A body…

"We have to get out of here."

He stared at her. "What?"

She grabbed his hand and pulled him toward the far end of the house.

At the front corner she hesitated, checked the street.

"Damn it." Neighbors were pouring out of their houses. The cops would be here soon.

He turned her around to face him. "We have to call the police."

"What we have to do," she fired back, her patience thinning, the words sounding a mile away, "is get the hell out of here."

She ran for the car. People pointed, shouted. She didn't understand the words, didn't care.

Her butt hit the driver's seat at the same time J.T. reached the driver's-side door.

"Get in the car," she ordered.

She started the engine, not caring whether he got in.

The car dipped with his weight, and she hit the accelerator.

A few seconds, tops, the police would be here. She and J.T. had to disappear before then. They couldn't investigate this case from behind bars.

The best way to get lost in a crowd of this size was in plain sight. She picked a side street and parked the car.

J.T. grabbed her hand to get her attention. "What are you *doing?*"

She shook her head, wishing the muffled sensation would go away. But she knew from experience it would take a few hours.

"We're going back to watch for your friend."

He stared a moment, an argument in his eyes. Then he got out and rounded the hood.

They took the side of the street lined with the most trees and shrubbery. As they reached the fringes of the crowd, they started pointing and asking questions just like everyone else.

Within another minute or so they had worked their way back to the house. The police had arrived, and crowd-control measures were in place.

Firefighters were preparing to hose down the flames.
Sirens wailing, lights throbbing.
But no sign of Ms. Rebecca James.
Eve folded her trembling arms over her chest.
The bitch had tried to kill them.

Chapter Fifteen

Crystal Lake, 8:30 p.m.

J.T. checked the perimeter of the cabin.

Clear.

He sat down on the front steps and heaved a breath. What the hell was going on? Rebecca hadn't shown. He'd tried to call her half a dozen times but had gotten her voice mail every time.

O'Brien had picked them up a few blocks from Arenas's house. Or what was left of it.

After he'd briefed Victoria, she had touched base with her contact at Chicago PD. She would give J.T. a heads-up on what was going on as soon as any information was available.

In the meantime he was to lay low.

His mother wouldn't be released from the hospital

until tomorrow. His colleagues had her under twenty-four-hour surveillance.

Victoria had assured him that he didn't need to worry about anything, how could he not?

His house had been invaded. A numbered account connected to serious embezzlement had been set up in his name. He'd been chased, shot at and nearly blown up.

And his mother had been beaten within an inch of her life.

After he'd had time to collect his thoughts, he'd realized that someone had to have been watching the house to know they'd gone inside. They'd been given time to get distracted by the body, and then the remote for the explosives had been triggered.

As big as the boom had felt up close, it hadn't been enough to destroy the house.

That hadn't been the intent.

The blast had been intended to kill or wound him badly enough to ensure he was discovered at the scene.

And Eve.

She had been a target, as well.

Yet she'd risked her life to ensure he got out first, which was another confusing element of the scenario. Why would she put his life before hers?

The same way, now that he thought about it, she

had at the warehouse. And at his house when he'd been ambushed on Friday night.

And what about her reaction, almost like jealousy, to Rebecca.

Was it possible she did have feelings for him?

He scrubbed a hand over his face. He was borrowing trouble. When this was over, she would be gone.

Just like before.

There were no words to accurately explain how he'd felt that day in the chapel when she hadn't shown. His whole world had felt as if it were ending.

The agony that night…the night they were supposed to have spent here…had paralyzed him.

Then he'd diverted all that pain into anger and the need to find the truth.

Had he found it? He still didn't even know her full name. Just Eve.

And yet he knew more about her after the past seventy-two hours than he had in two months…before.

"Whatever."

He pushed to his feet.

Tonight he needed to get some sleep so he could take care of business tomorrow. He had to find some answers. And he had to take care of his mother.

Eve…would take care of herself. She'd definitely proved capable of doing that.

He went inside, closed and locked the door.

She was standing by the kitchen island. He froze.

With her hair damp, she wore nothing but a towel. Her long, toned legs made his throat ache. The creamy skin of her shoulders enticed him for a taste.

"Sorry. I thought you were outside." She gestured to the sink. "I was thirsty."

He held up a hand. "It's okay. I need a shower anyway."

Without a backward glance, which wasn't an easy feat, he strode to the bedroom. He crossed to the en suite bath and closed the door. Her discarded clothes were scattered over the floor. Jeans. T-shirt. Skimpy panties.

He focused his attention on setting the water temperature.

After he'd stripped off his clothes, he climbed into the shower. The hot spray of water felt good on his sore muscles. The impact with the ground had left him achy. But they were both damned lucky to survive with nothing but a few bruises.

Damned lucky.

He stood beneath the hot spray for a while after he'd gone through the cleaning ritual. His body needed the heat…. Or maybe he was just avoiding Eve.

When the water started to cool, he shut it off and climbed out.

Eve was standing in the open door. She thrust a pair of jeans at him. "I thought you might need these."

The towel was gone.

His gaze traveled the length of her naked body, then lifted to meet hers.

"Thanks." He reached out, accepted the jeans.

She didn't move.

He didn't move.

"You…" She licked her lips.

His throat tightened, his chest squeezed.

"You were a mistake," she confessed.

He flinched and felt the pain radiate down his body.

She shook her head. "I don't mean the way you think." She drew in a big breath, and her chest expanded, lifting her firm breasts…drawing his attention to pert, soft nipples he longed to touch.

"I was wrong to let things go so far." She looked away. "I should have maintained better control, kept it simple." Her gaze lifted to his. "I hurt you and I didn't mean to."

He dropped the jeans, took a step in her direction. "Things have been out of control since the day we met." He couldn't deny that. She wasn't the only one who had let things go too far.

She stood very still. Let him close in on her.

"You—" she looked up at him "—don't know me. I don't even know me."

He touched her hair. He loved her hair. So long, thick…beautiful. He loved to feel it between his fingers…gliding over his skin. "I know this." He bent his head down, pressed his lips to hers.

Her taste, the feel of her lips, awakened his senses as nothing else could. He traced the seam of her lips with his tongue, wanting to be inside her. She opened for him, drew him in.

His arms went around her narrow waist, pulled her body to his damp one. He groaned at the heat of her skin, the silky softness of her body compared with his hard-muscled frame. She fit against him perfectly.

The kiss went on and on until they melted together. He lifted her against his chest, scooped her into his arms and carried her to the bed.

He laid her down gently, her head resting on the pillow, her sleek body arranged languidly on the crisp white linens.

She was so beautiful.

She held her hand out to him. He laced his fingers with hers and pressed his palm to hers.

With one firm tug she pulled him down on the bed beside her. Neither of them cared that he was still damp from the shower. He didn't hurry. He took his time. He wanted to touch every part of her, to authenticate every memory already imprinted on his very soul.

EVE KNEW SHE SHOULDN'T allow this to happen. But she couldn't resist his touch. She needed this one night with him.

The concept of stopping was unthinkable.

No one had ever touched her the way J.T. did. Making love with him had been like making love for the first time. He'd brought the woman in her to an emotional pinnacle she hadn't known existed.

He'd given himself completely, had offered her his entire being.

Not once in her life had she ever wanted that much of anyone.

But she wanted it now. At least for tonight.

His fingers trailed down her torso, tracing, teasing, tempting.

He kissed her throat, followed the same path his fingers had taken with his lips. He circled one taunt nipple, tugged on it with his teeth, then sank fully onto it, drawing it into his hot mouth.

She moaned and lost herself to his touch until they were one. He moved inside her, filling her completely. Nothing mattered then. Not the past…not the future.

There was only now and the way he could blur it all with his tenderness.

This would prove her biggest mistake of all.

Not the making love…but the thinking she could just walk away.

Chapter Sixteen

Chicago, 11:30 p.m.

Victoria sat on the side of her granddaughter's bed. The child slept so peacefully, without a care in the world. So trusting.

She would not see that taken from her granddaughter, not the way it had been taken from her son. Victoria closed her eyes and fought back the memories. She failed miserably; the memories came in a deluge. The misery that accompanied each one making it impossible to breathe normally.

Jim had been seven years old, barely a year older than Jamie was now, when evil had snatched him away.

Errol Leberman.

The devil himself.

He'd taken Victoria's child and tried his best to turn him into a monster. He'd kept Jim chained in a basement for years, treated him like an animal, tortured him physically and mentally. Then he'd sent the child away to serve as a slave at a mercenary training camp.

Victoria had read the psychiatric reports during Jim's treatment and recovery. It was only by the grace of God the boy had survived the horrors he had suffered.

But he had survived. Victoria gathered her courage around her. As had she. Her son was a good, strong man now with a wonderful wife and a beautiful daughter.

Victoria would not allow this child to suffer those trials. She would protect her.

No matter the cost.

Merri had been right about Jamie's favorite toy. A cutting-edge tracking device had been added to each of the stuffed bear's eyes. The manufacturer had been unable to trace the serial numbers to a buyer. The paper trail had been so muddled that determining the source had been utterly impossible.

The question now was how had anyone gained access to the toy in the first place? The bear was always one of two places, at Victoria's home or in Jamie's arms. Since the toy wasn't permitted at school, it was only with Jamie when she was with Victoria or a member of her staff. There was never an opportunity for it to fall into the enemy's hands.

Unless the tracking devices were, as Ian and

Simon suggested, integrated at some prior date. Before Jim and Tasha had left for their vacation.

Which meant that the threat had been planned well in advance and had been carried out by an intimate.

Someone Jim and Tasha knew…well enough to trust the person in their daughter's presence.

Or in their home.

Chapter Seventeen

Crystal Lake, 1:00 a.m.

Eve sat on the end of the bed watching J.T. sleep. But she couldn't sleep, not until this was done.

Eve had told herself over and over that this ultimately would have happened, with or without her involvement.

But that didn't absolve her conscience.

If she had turned down this job, perhaps J.T. would not have gotten dragged into this dangerous game of blame and kill.

His superior, Victoria Colby-Camp, had called. The police wanted J.T. to come in for questioning. He planned to go at nine this morning.

Next Rebecca James would make her move. She would report the fraud and point a finger at J.T. He wasn't totally convinced of that scenario just yet, but Eve knew. She had no proof, but she knew.

She'd sensed something sinister in the woman. That didn't make her smarter or better at reading people than J.T.; it only proved her pathetic childhood had been good for something.

Eve's aunt had been like Rebecca James. She showed one side of herself to those who could provide some advantage or opportunity. But in other settings with those who offered nothing of consequence, she turned into an evil bitch.

Rebecca was the one behind this high-stakes game. There was no way to know for sure how she had persuaded Terrence Arenas to go along with her.

Sex? Money? Both maybe.

Eve had narrowed down her theories to two: either Rebecca was planning to stay and ensure that J.T. and/or Arenas were charged with her crimes, or the whole situation was a smokescreen until Rebecca could get her ducks in a row and disappear.

Eve couldn't speculate as to Damon Howe's involvement—if any—in the scenario.

Rebecca had had a good thing going for quite a while, maybe longer than they knew. What had made her take these abrupt measures? Had someone caught on to her scam? Paula Jamison? Maybe Arenas himself?

Or had Jamison's threat of legal action been the straw that broke the camel's back?

One thing was certain—the usual methods wouldn't get to the bottom of what had gone down. Rebecca would lie. She'd likely taken great pains to cover her tracks. It would be her word against J.T.'s. The court proceedings could take years. His legal fees would mount. All for nothing more than to prove his innocence.

The only way to get to the truth was to extract it in a manner the bitch would understand.

The police weren't going to do that: it was illegal.

J.T. and the Colby Agency might bend the rules, but they would never break them.

Eve walked a different line when it came to rules and laws. She would do whatever it took.

All she needed was a weapon.

Facing the enemy unarmed and unprepared was just stupid.

She eased off the bed and went in search of her shoes and the keys to their borrowed car.

J.T. had a weapon at his place.

The only caveat was getting in and out without getting caught.

Chicago, 2:30 a.m.

J.T.'S HOUSE WAS DARK. The garage door was closed. Someone from the Colby Agency had come by and secured the place.

But Eve knew where he kept his spare key.

She made her way through the dark to the barbecue grill. Beneath the gas grill's fuel tank was the key. With it clasped in her hand, she hurried across the backyard and to the rear entrance.

As soon as the door was open, she entered the security code to deactivate the system and stop the chime that signaled the alarm was armed.

Moving through the darkness, she made her way to his bedroom. He kept his Beretta on the top shelf of the closet beneath a handful of baseball caps. She grabbed the holstered weapon and an extra ammo clip.

Taking advantage of the resources available, Eve packed a plastic shopping bag with certain necessities and checked J.T.'s home-office Rolodex for the address she needed. She then hurried out of the house, rearming the security system as she went.

After loading back into the car and driving away, she realized that the fact that she didn't encounter the enemy was yet another indication the game was winding down. The enemy was confident enough in its position that it was no longer maintaining all levels of surveillance. It now boiled down to whether J.T. could hold his own with Rebecca James.

Eve drove straight to the Lincoln Park address and determined her strategy.

A sign near the stoop indicated there was a security system. Eve didn't have the necessary equipment on hand to deactivate it. All she had was the few items she'd collected at J.T.'s.

Ground-floor windows were all locked. From the kitchen window she could see that the security system was armed. Great.

Going in through one of the doors was out of the question. Few people bothered with the home security window strips, only the glass breaks. Break a window and the alarm was triggered. Raise a window and nothing.

Didn't matter in this case. The windows were locked, and without the necessary tools they were going to stay that way.

Then Eve spotted a lucky break: A doggie door in the garage door.

Putting her bag through first, she wiggled through the hinged door. Inside the garage, she pulled out her flashlight and had a look around. The door was a lucky break, but the pet for which it was installed might not be so. After a careful survey of the garage, she felt secure there was no need to worry. No dog food.

Then she spotted the massive bag of cat food. Not a doggie door, a cat door.

The door leading from the garage into the house would no doubt be a part of the security network. Again, luck was with Eve. Another pet door. All she had to do was wiggle through without jarring the entry door's magnetic strip loose from its connector strip.

Slowly Eve inched her shoulders, then her torso, through the little swinging door. She had to angle her hips to get them through. She held her breath, praying that she didn't disturb the contact.

Relief washed over her as she scooted onto her hands and knees in the kitchen.

Two lucky breaks in a row. That wouldn't hold out.

Eve tucked the Beretta into her waistband and deposited on the kitchen counter the other tools she'd brought along. She walked quietly through the house until she found the owner's suite.

Moonlight filtered in through the blinds, providing just enough light for Eve to make her way through the room without tripping over anything.

Thankfully Rebecca James was alone.

Eve wrapped her fingers around the butt of the Beretta and moved in close to the sleeping woman.

She'd just opened her mouth to spout an order to get up, when Rebecca rolled to her back and stuck a Ruger in her face.

"Don't you dare move," Rebecca threatened. "I will blow your head off."

Crystal Lake, 3:00 a.m.

J.T. SAT STRAIGHT UP. Something was wrong.

He surveyed the room. Where was Eve?

He threw the sheet back and crossed to the bathroom.

No Eve.

He checked the living room and kitchen.

With dread settling like a rock on his chest, he checked the porch and yard.

No Eve.

No car.

"Damn it." He rushed back to the bedroom and tugged on his jeans and shoes. He grabbed his T-shirt and the keys to his bike.

He knew where she would be.

Eve was convinced Rebecca was the one behind Gold Cost Life's fraud. Obviously she'd decided to prove her theory.

If Rebecca was desperate enough to set this bizarre chain of events in motion, she was desperate enough to do anything.

Even commit murder.

Two men and one woman were already dead.

Chapter Eighteen

"You should have stayed gone." Rebecca shook her head and made that annoying tsk sound as she paced her living room. "Then everything would have worked out exactly as planned."

"That's why you always have a backup plan," Eve advised.

Rebecca waved the Ruger in Eve's face. "Really? I doubt any kind of plan is going to save you now."

"Maybe you're right." Eve relaxed in the chair Rebecca had secured her to. She wasn't very good at tying knots. Eve had almost worked free the ones holding her hands behind the chair. It did kind of tick her off that she'd used the nylon rope Eve had brought with her.

"I guess Terrence's backup plan didn't save him.

Or his property caretaker." Maybe J.T. wasn't convinced, but Eve was absolutely certain that Rebecca had killed them both.

"I thought using your gun was a nice touch." Rebecca tapped the barrel of the Ruger against her chin. "Even if it was damaged in the explosion, they can do amazing things with evidence analysis these days."

"How do you know your hired help won't do the same to you that you did to Terrence?" Eve didn't really care about the answer. She was just buying time. Keeping her talking. "I counted at least five men on your team."

"They don't know anything. Contract workers. The kind that will do anything for money and never ask questions. They're long gone by now. Moved on to the next job—just as you should have done." She laughed. "Did you really think he was worth coming back here for? A man like J.T. would never settle for a con artist like you."

Fury ignited low in Eve's belly. "I guess he didn't fall for you, either."

Rebecca smiled. "I never intended it to be anything more than a one-night stand. I sealed his trust that night. My focus was on prodding Terrence to take care of business."

"What'd you promise him? A happily ever after?"

For a guy twenty-five years her senior and likely very lonely, that had to be a tempting offer.

"In paradise no less," Rebecca confirmed. "The Caymans. He wanted to buy a boat and fish all day." She rolled her eyes. "As if."

"How could he have expected to end up with a woman like you?" Eve said aloud what Rebecca was no doubt thinking. "Terrence had to know that it was about the money."

"Really. That old bag Jamison was more his speed. He let her get to him; she had him feeling so sorry for her." Rebecca smirked. "A very bad move on his part."

"He probably never saw it coming," Eve suggested, wanting details. The police would need details to clear J.T.

"Absolutely not. He liked all those kinky sex games." She shuddered. "Getting him to try the whole asphyxiation thing was a piece of cake. Then I just kicked the chair out from under him so to speak. Too bad."

Eve flinched. She stiffened to ensure she didn't let her arms sag. Her hands were free. There was no way to free her ankles. She would just have to work with what she had. "Who was the man who gave me my instructions?" she prodded. "Obviously it wasn't Terrence."

"Actually it was. I found you on the Internet, and he acted as your point of contact. Of course, the last call wasn't from him. That was me."

"Voice changer?"

"State-of-the-art," Rebecca explained. "You can order anything on the Internet these days. When it became necessary to make that final call to you, I worked at the settings until I was satisfied. And it worked exactly as planned."

Eve laughed. "So, you're the one who failed to disconnect."

Fury whipped across the other woman's face. "What are you talking about?"

"The debrief we held," Eve reminded her. "The final call. When you ended the call, you didn't disconnect. That's how I knew what you had planned for J.T."

Rebecca tilted her chin in defiance of the accusation. "Oh well. Your showing back up just gave me the opportunity to clean up one last loose end."

"Oh well," Eve echoed. She had to wait for the right moment, that fleeting opportunity that would make all the difference.

"I think for you," Rebecca said, "I'll shoot you in that pretty face. Then untie you, of course, and fire a couple shots from your Beretta—using your hand just to make sure all the bases are covered. When the authorities arrive, I'll tell them how you broke into my house. I'm sure they'll find trace fibers where you crawled through the pet doors. You attacked me and I retaliated—end of story. You and J.T. knew I was onto your scam. His calls to me will document my statements."

"Too bad J.T. wasn't invited to this little party," Eve suggested. "Then you could kill two birds with one stone."

"Oh, he'll get his," Rebecca said, certain of herself. "Someone has to go to jail for ripping off all those poor souls. It might as well be him."

What a bitch.

"The problem as I see it," Eve said, "is that your backup plan is a little thin. Anemic, even."

"How do you figure that? You're here all tied up. I have the gun." She waved the Ruger. "I'm weary of the chitchat, so why don't we see who has the best plan?"

"I guess you didn't factor in J.T. showing up uninvited." Eve sent a pointed glance at the door behind Rebecca.

When Rebecca looked back, Eve took that one fleeting opportunity. She propelled herself toward the woman and head butted her with every ounce of strength she possessed.

The Ruger clattered to the floor. Fingers burrowed deep into Eve's hair. Eve went for her throat.

Rebecca twisted. They hit the floor in a tangle of arms, legs and chair.

Eve scrambled for the weapon.

Rebecca got to it first.

Eve swung her forearm upward, hitting the barrel of the weapon pointed in her face.

A bullet exploded from the muzzle. It whizzed past her head and plowed into the hardwood floor.

No way was Eve going to let this bitch kill her.

Eve's arms shook as she attempted to swing the barrel away from her face once more.

"Rebecca!"

J.T.'s voice echoed in the room.

Both women froze.

"It's over, Rebecca," J.T. warned.

The other woman's gaze remained locked on Eve's. Neither moved nor even dared to breathe.

"The police know everything," he went on. "It's over."

Rebecca's face twisted. A scream exploded from her lips. She abruptly rolled free of Eve, scrambled to her feet and leveled her weapon on J.T.

Her ankles still bound, Eve lost her balance when she attempted to get to her feet. By the time she was standing, the reality of the situation had sunk into her brain.

J.T had come…unarmed.

The Ruger was leveled on his chest.

Eve held her breath, railed at her brain to come up with a plan. A way to turn this around.

"Just put the gun down," J.T. urged gently. "That won't change anything now. The Colby Agency traced the Cayman account and the dummy corporation back to Terrence, who had listed you as a shareholder. The truth is out. It's over."

Eve wanted to look at J.T., but she couldn't take her eyes off Rebecca. The look of desperation in her eyes, the determined expression on her face, foreshadowed what would happen next.

Surrender was not an option.

"You're right," Rebecca said, her voice abruptly calm, her face suddenly relaxed. "It is over. For you."

Eve launched herself at the other woman.

The weapon fired.

They crashed together against the stone hearth.

Pain registered in Eve's skull. She grimaced.

Think!

Where was the gun? What was wrong with her?

The room shifted. Blackness narrowed Eve's vision.

J.T. called her name.

Had he been hit?

Or maybe she had....

Chapter Nineteen

Colby Agency, 9:15 a.m.

Victoria dropped her purse behind her desk. She was exhausted. The last several hours had been spent at the Mercy General E.R.

Perhaps another cup of coffee would pep her up.

Poor J.T. Victoria shook her head.

The nightmare—

"Victoria."

Simon's voice boomed in the room a split second before he burst through the door.

Victoria squared her shoulders, focused her weary attention on the man who was clearly disturbed. "Is there news from the hospital?" She'd only just left. Surely nothing else—

Simon held up a hand for her to wait. "Ian is transferring a call to your desk."

What on earth was he talking about? Fear detonated in Victoria's veins. "Jamie?" The name was a harsh whisper on her lips. Merri and Jane had taken Jamie to school together. Two of Victoria's best men had accompanied them. Jane had confirmed that Jamie was in her classroom and all was well. Jane would remain inside the school for the duration of the day. Two more of Victoria's staff would continue surveillance outside the school. Surely nothing had happened in those few minutes.

"No, no," Simon urged. "Jamie is fine. A call came in," he explained. "Ian is—"

"I've routed the call to your conference table," Ian announced as he entered Victoria's office. He closed the door behind him. "The call is set to be recorded. We're ready when you are."

Simon gestured for her to have a seat at the head of her conference table.

Victoria moved to take the seat. "I'm confused. Who's on the line?" Her first thought was Lucas or Jim. But there wouldn't be any reason to record a call from either of them.

"The man who claims responsibility for the abduction attempts," Ian explained. "He says he has an offer for you."

When Simon and Ian had taken their seats, Victoria reached for the button that would open the call to the conference table's speaker system.

"This is Victoria Colby-Camp." Her voice sounded strong despite the trembling rampant inside her.

"Ah, Victoria."

She analyzed the voice. Didn't recognize it. "Identify yourself, sir."

A vile laugh echoed through the speakers.

A chill swept over Victoria.

"I'm going to leave that up to you to determine," the voice said. "I will, however, give you a number of clues to my identity."

Simon reached for a notepad and poised his pen in preparation for taking notes.

"You've overestimated your ability to hold my attention," Victoria warned. "State your business, or this conversation is over."

Silence radiated in the air. Five seconds…ten.

Anxiety tightened in Victoria's throat. Had her move been too bold?

"We had a mutual friend," he offered smugly. "He had a tremendous influence on your son's life."

The fear turned to stone cold terror.

"Errol Leberman told me many things about you and your two husbands as well as your agency. I will say that I'm rather disappointed your brilliant staff has been unable to find me, or even to identify me.

That said, I'm still willing to do business. I can tolerate incompetence as long as the price is right."

"Get to the point." Victoria would not be baited by this man.

"I will call off the planned abduction of your precious granddaughter for the sum of ten million dollars. That full amount will be electronically deposited in an account of my choosing."

Startled by the man's blunt offer, Victoria looked from Ian to Simon. Their faces reflected the same astonishment.

"Speechless, I see," the voice taunted.

Victoria took a moment, weighed her options and made her decision. "Again, you overestimate yourself, sir. First, be warned that my people will find you. Perhaps not today, but soon."

"I would," he warned with swaggering arrogance, "tread with caution—"

"I am not finished yet," Victoria interrupted, her determination mounting in tandem with his arrogance. "We will find you. So, *you* tread cautiously, sir. Secondly, the Colby Agency does not negotiate with terrorists. And you, sir, are a terrorist. Stay away from my family, or you will end up exactly like your friend Leberman."

Victoria hit the button, ending the call.

For a long moment Ian and Simon said nothing.

Uncertainty suddenly thumped hard inside Victoria. Or perhaps it was her racing heart.

"You did well, Victoria." Ian gave her an acknowledging nod. "I couldn't have said it better myself."

"I agree," Simon chimed in. "However," he looked from Victoria to Ian and back, "we must be vigilant. This is far from over. Our position may make him more determined to accomplish his goal."

Unfortunately Simon was correct.

The threat was by no means over.

At least now they had a voice…and confirmation that the threat was from the past, history that had already been written and couldn't be undone.

Colby history.

Victoria stood. "I need coffee." She lifted her chin in defiance of her own quivering emotions. "And an update from the hospital."

Victoria would deal with this threat the same way she did all threats: one step, one day at a time, until it was neutralized.

She needed Jim back here. He might recognize the voice of the caller.

She paused at the door and turned to Ian. "Try to get my son on the line. We can't hold off on contacting him any longer. Maybe he can identify that voice."

Victoria squared her shoulders and walked out of her office. Evidently this threat had its roots in Leberman. One or more of his scattered minions had chosen to carry on his twisted legacy. To stir up the past once more. To start the war again.

This time Victoria was going to end it.

For good.

Chapter Twenty

J.T. paced the room. What was taking so long?

To his relief the door opened. The nurse pushed the wheelchair into the room. Eve sat slumped in the rolling chair, a stark white bandage on her forehead.

J.T.'s fears and anxiety lifted a fraction. "How'd it go?"

"It went," Eve grumbled.

"She has a nasty concussion," the nurse said as she assisted Eve into the waiting bed. "The doctor will be in soon to go over his findings."

"I'm ready to get out of here," Eve stated.

"We'll have to see what the doctor says, Ms. Mattson," the nurse reminded before hurrying back to her station.

J.T. moved to the bedside and surveyed Eve for the

hundredth time. "How's the pain?" The doctor wouldn't order a painkiller until they understood the severity of the head injury.

"What do you think?" Eve growled. "It stinks."

J.T. had to smile. The way she was complaining, she had to be okay.

When that gun had fired the second time, he'd thought he would lose his mind until he determined that Eve wasn't hit. He'd quickly realized that the headfirst ram into the rock hearth had done some serious damage. The struggle over the gun with Rebecca that had followed still made J.T.'s teeth grind. He'd managed to gain control of the weapon and to subdue her at the same time.

Thankfully he'd had the foresight to put in a call to Ian en route. The police had shown up within minutes of J.T.'s arrival at Rebecca's home. Paramedics had gotten to the scene in record time.

Rebecca's criminal activity would be sorted out soon. J.T. wasn't completely out of the woods with the authorities, but with the Colby Agency's help, that would be resolved in time.

For now, his only concern was Eve.

"In case I haven't told you," he said as he settled on the edge of the bed next to her, "thanks for saving my life."

Eve sighed. "You said that already."

Another smile tugged at J.T.'s lips. "I guess you won't be able to collect the rest of your fee, considering you helped bring down your employer."

"Truth is, I'd already been paid in full. Even if I hadn't been, it wouldn't be a big deal."

She wouldn't look at him. He understood the tactic—she didn't want him reading her eyes.

He toyed with the hem of her gown. "When you're released, you'll be on your way, I suppose." Holding his breath, he focused on her face to wait for the answer. He wanted to see what she was feeling. He needed to see…to know.

"I suppose."

Still no eye contact. But her voice spoke volumes. Too quiet. Too subdued. Not Eve at all.

"You could stay," he ventured.

Her gaze shifted to his. "Why would I stay?"

This was the moment. The one where he had to take that leap of faith, no matter that she'd let him down before. She had her reasons. Reasons he didn't understand, but their lives had been different. He couldn't hold that against her.

"Because I—" he hesitated "—I want you to stay. I still have that wedding ring and the fancy tux." He shrugged. "It would be a shame to waste them."

"You don't even know my full name," she argued, showing some of that strength he recognized.

He took her hand in his and felt it tremble ever so slightly. "So what's your name?"

Five, six, ten seconds ticked off.

"Evelyn Shelby. I was born in Winnetka. I moved to Phoenix when my parents died."

His heart lurched. That she'd opened up to him that little bit was a major milestone. "So this is home. Sort of."

"Sort of." She stared at their joined hands now.

"Then staying here would be like coming home," he offered.

She searched his eyes, hers carefully shielded. "I'm not the person you think I am," she warned. "I've lived on the edge of the law for most of my adult life. There are risks involved with having me in your life. The past could come back to haunt me. Change might not work for me." She blinked, tried to keep the uncertainty hidden but failed. "You should think long and hard about taking on all that baggage."

"I've already thought about it." He squeezed her hand. "I'm prepared to accept the challenge. That is…if you're up to it. If you're afraid…" He let the challenge hang in the air.

The ghost of a smile played across her gorgeous lips. "I'm not afraid of anything, J. T. Baxley. Never have been."

"I'll take that as a yes." He leaned down, brushed his lips across hers.

"Definitely." She reached up, traced his lips with a fingertip. "Yes."

There would be potholes ahead, J.T. was certain, but the destination would be more than worth the bumpy ride.

* * * * *

Look for the conclusion of
COLBY AGENCY:
ELITE RECONNAISSANCE DIVISION
next month!
Here's a sneak peek of
HIS SECRET LIFE
by
Debra Webb

Colby Agency, 2:00 p.m.

Victoria Colby-Camp collected her purse and prepared to order the car. Picking up her granddaughter at school would definitely be the highlight of this day.

After spending a good portion of the morning at the E.R. with J.T. and Eve, then dealing with that unnerving call from the bastard behind the abduction attempts, Victoria had long passed exhaustion.

She needed Lucas at her side. The government contact that served as a liaison whenever Lucas was on assignment had been unable to reach him or any member of his team. The reason, of course, was classified. Victoria had put off reaching out to Lucas as long as she dared.

She could no longer presume the threat to her

granddaughter was minimal. With that call the danger had escalated to a new level.

The past had come back to haunt the Colby Agency once more.

An associate of Errol Leberman, the arch nemesis of the Colby name, was behind the threat. Victoria had not recognized the caller's voice. He had refused to give his name, pushing Victoria into a corner and limiting her options to the two she had hoped to avoid: reaching out to Lucas and to Jim.

The past two years her son had taken great strides in settling into a normal, happy life. Jim and his wife, Tasha, were immensely happy and their daughter, Jamie, thrived. This extended vacation to the darkest depths of Africa was the couple's first getaway. Victoria had not wanted to disturb their escape. Her son so deserved to take a real vacation for the first time in his life, to experience an adventure that was for pure enjoyment and not related to his work.

But the caller and the situation had left her no choice.

Since she'd been forced to reach out to Lucas, her people had been attempting to reach Jim all day.

He and Tasha were in a remote part of Africa. Recent political unrest had concerned Victoria as to their selection of this safari for their getaway. Tasha had great empathy for the continent and its many woes. She had chosen the place for that reason. Jim had agreed. Victoria had reminded herself that her son was more than capable of taking care of himself and his wife in any situation. There had been no need to worry.

But that had been before. Before rumors surfaced that Jamie Colby was a target. Before they had been ambushed and three people had lost their lives.

Before the call.

Victoria shuddered as memories of Leberman and the horrors he had used against the Colby name crowded into her thoughts. Any people associated with him would be every bit as evil and twisted. Worse, they would go to any lengths to accomplish their mission.

The possibility of their success terrified Victoria.

She swallowed back the emotions that constricted her throat. Victoria had never allowed anyone or anything to shake her confidence and determination to this degree.

But this absolutely shook her to the core.

Perhaps she was not as strong as she once was.

Her office door opened, snapping her to attention.

"We have Jim on the line," Ian Michaels announced.

Simon Ruhl came in behind him and closed the door.

A mixture of relief and anticipation seared Victoria's senses. "Finally."

They moved to the conference table, where Ian activated the conferencing system. "Jim, Simon and I are in Victoria's offices. Are you in a position to speak at length?"

"For as long as the connection lasts," Jim replied.

Emotion surged upon hearing her son's voice. Victoria smiled even as tears welled in her eyes. "Jim, it's good to hear your voice."

"What's wrong? I can hear the worry in *your* voice, Victoria."

Victoria had hoped that at some point her son would feel comfortable calling her, "mother," but that hadn't happened yet. Years of brainwashing and bitterness had made any sort of intimacy on a normal level difficult. Still, their relationship was close, solid.

"There's a situation," she explained, annoyed that her voice quavered. "We had hoped to contain the threat without interfering with your vacation, but that has changed now."

"Tell me," Jim commanded, his tone fierce, tight, "that my daughter is safe."

"Jamie is safe—" Victoria hurried to assure him. "She is unharmed and having a grand time being the center of attention. We have the maximum security measures in place. For now, all is under control where her welfare is concerned."

"There's been a threat against her," Jim surmised.

His voice had lost all inflection. When threatened, he closed out all emotions, a tactic he'd learned after years of abuse. Agony twisted in Victoria. She would give most anything not to have to do this to him.

"Yes," she confirmed. "Ian is going to bring you up to speed."

Surprised, Ian shifted his attention to her, and Victoria nodded for him to take the reins. She did not trust herself to maintain her composure.

She looked away as Ian launched into the details of the threat to her granddaughter. More of those stinging emotions burned in her eyes. Inside, where no one could see, she trembled.

For the first time in a very long time she was afraid. Uncertain of herself.

Leberman had reached out from the grave and done this to her.

The bastard.

"Victoria."

She blinked and returned her focus to the two men seated at the conference table with her. "Yes?" She mentally scrambled to catch up. Had Ian asked her a question?

"Jim is ready to listen to the recording."

She nodded. "Of course."

Ian gave Simon a nod. Simon initiated the playback of the recorded call.

Victoria put her hands in her lap and clasped them tightly as the sinister voice filled the room.

When the recording had reached an end, the silence thickened for several moments before Jim spoke.

"His name is Clayton Barker. He operated the mercenary camp where I stayed for two years. Do not underestimate him. If he's behind this…"

Victoria heard talking in the background. One voice sounded like Tasha's.

"Jim?" A new kind of tension quivered through Victoria. The background conversation sounded clipped, tense.

"Look," Jim said, apparently moving away from the conversation in the background, since the voices faded. "I'm coming home. I don't know how long it will take. There's been some trouble here."

More of that paralyzing fear streamed through Victoria's veins. "Related to the political climate?"

"Yes," Jim confirmed. "We thought we were safe, but trouble has moved into this area. We were already preparing to move out before your call was patched through. Tasha and I will head back to Kenya and get on the first flight back home."

"Can we get a helicopter to your location to facilitate your departure?" Ian suggested.

"Won't work. The government has shut down all air traffic in the area. We'll have to try getting out in the Jeeps. If that doesn't work, we'll do it on foot. I will get there, one way or another."

"Jim—" Victoria worked at keeping her voice even "—are you and Tasha safe for now?"

"For now." His tone was grave.

Adrenaline fired through Victoria, and she snatched back her crumbling resolve and courage. "Listen to me, Jim," she said, her voice stronger than before, "you take care of yourself and your wife. Make your way back here, but don't take unnecessary risks. All of us are working on this situation. We will find Barker, and we will do whatever is necessary to stop him. Jamie will be protected. Do not doubt that for a moment. You have my word."

She'd lost it for a moment, but there was no way Victoria Colby-Camp was going to be undone by a lowlife like Barker. She would prevail. She looked from Ian to Simon. She had the best of the best behind her.

"I know you will do all you can," Jim said, "but I can't risk that it might not be enough. I'm coming back. Nothing here will stop me."

The call ended with one last plea from Victoria for him to take care.

He needn't worry—she would not let him down. Not again.

As much as she understood that her son loved her

and that his words were not a reflection of her failure, she knew what his statement meant.

Victoria had done all within her power to keep Jim safe as a child.

And it hadn't been enough.

* * * * *

RICK'S APPOINTMENT with his attorney early Wednesday morning went only moderately better than his meeting with social services the day before. The prognosis wasn't great—but at least his attorney was going to file a motion for DNA testing. Just so Rick could petition to see the child…his sister's baby. The sister he didn't know he had until it was too late.

The rest of what his attorney said had been downhill from there.

Cell phone in hand before he'd even reached his Nitro, Rick punched in the speed-dial number he'd programmed the day before.

Maybe foster parent Sue Bookman hadn't received his message. Or had lost his number. Maybe she didn't want to talk to him. At this point he didn't much care what she wanted.

"Hello?" She answered before the first ring was complete. And sounded breathless.

Young and breathless.

"Ms. Bookman?"

"Yes. This is Rick Kraynick, right?"

"Yes, ma'am."

"I recognized your number on caller ID," she said, her voice uneven, as though she was still engaged in whatever physical activity had her so breathless to begin with. "I'm sorry I didn't get back to you. I've been a little…distracted."

The words came in more disjointed spurts. Was she jogging?

"No problem," he said, when, in fact, he'd spent the better part of the night before watching his phone. And fretting. "Did I get you at a bad time?"

"No worse than usual," she said, adding, "Better than some. So, how can I help?"

God, if only this could be so easy. He'd ask. She'd help. And life could go well. At least for one little person in his family.

It would be a first.

"Mr. Kraynick?"

"Yes. Sorry. I was…are you sure there isn't a better time to call?"

"I'm bouncing a baby, Mr. Kraynick. It's what I do."

"Is it Carrie?" he asked quickly, his pulse racing.

"How do you know Carrie?" She sounded defensive, which wouldn't do him any good.

"I'm her uncle," he explained, "her mother's—Christy's—older brother, and I know you have her."

"I can neither confirm nor deny your allegations, Mr. Kraynick. Please call social services." She rattled off the number.

"Wait!" he said, unable to hide his urgency. "Please," he said more calmly. "Just hear me out."

"How did you find me?"

"A friend of Christy's."

"I'm sorry I can't help you, Mr. Kraynick," she said softly. "This conversation is over."

"I grew up in foster care," he said, as though that gave him some special privilege. Some insider's edge.

"Then you know you shouldn't be calling me at all."

"Yes… But Carrie is my niece," he said. "I need to see her. To know that she's okay."

"You'll have to go through social services to arrange that."

"I'm sure you know it's not as easy as it sounds. I'm a single man with no real ties and I've no intention of petitioning for custody. They aren't real eager to give me the time of day. I never even knew Carrie's mother. For all intents and purposes, our mother didn't raise either one of us. All I have going for me is half a set of genes. My lawyer's on it, but it could be weeks—months—before this is sorted out. Carrie could be adopted by then. Which would be fine, great

for her, but then I'd have lost my chance. I don't want
to take her. I won't hurt her. I just have to see her."

"I'm sorry, Mr. Kraynick, but…"

* * * * *

Find out if Rick Kraynick will ever have
a chance to meet his niece.
Look for A DAUGHTER'S TRUST
by Tara Taylor Quinn,
available in September 2009.

We'll be spotlighting a different series
every month throughout 2009
to celebrate our 60th anniversary.

**Look for Harlequin® Superromance®
in September!**

*Celebrate with
The Diamond Legacy
miniseries!*

Follow the stories of four cousins as they come to terms
with the complications of love and what it means to
be a family. Discover with them the sixty-year-old secret
that rocks not one but two families.

A DAUGHTER'S TRUST by *Tara Taylor Quinn*
September

FOR THE LOVE OF FAMILY by *Kathleen O'Brien*
October

LIKE FATHER, LIKE SON by *Karina Bliss*
November

A MOTHER'S SECRET by *Janice Kay Johnson*
December

Available wherever books are sold.

You're invited to join our Tell Harlequin Reader Panel!

By joining our new reader panel you will:

- Receive Harlequin® books—they are FREE and yours to keep with no obligation to purchase anything!
- Participate in fun online surveys
- Exchange opinions and ideas with women just like you
- Have a say in our new book ideas and help us publish the best in women's fiction

In addition, you will have a chance to win great prizes and receive special gifts! See Web site for details. Some conditions apply. Space is limited.

To join, visit us at
www.TellHarlequin.com.

REQUEST YOUR FREE BOOKS!

2 FREE NOVELS PLUS 2 FREE GIFTS!

HARLEQUIN®
INTRIGUE®

Breathtaking Romantic Suspense

Stay up-to-date on all your romance reading news!

The Harlequin Inside Romance newsletter is a **FREE** quarterly newsletter highlighting our upcoming series releases and promotions!

Go to
eHarlequin.com/InsideRomance
or e-mail us at
InsideRomance@Harlequin.com
to sign up to receive
your **FREE** newsletter today!

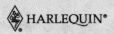

#1155 SMOKIN' SIX-SHOOTER by B.J. Daniels
Whitehorse, Montana: The Corbetts

Although her new neighbor is all cowboy, she isn't looking for love—she wants answers to an unsolved murder. But when she digs too deep and invites the attention of a killer, her cowboy may be all that stands between her and a certain death.

#1156 AN UNEXPECTED CLUE by Elle James
Kenner County Crime Unit

When his cover is blown, the undercover FBI agent fears for the life of his wife and the child she carries. Although she no longer trusts him, he'll do whatever he has to do to save her and win back her love.

#1157 HIS SECRET LIFE by Debra Webb
Colby Agency: Elite Reconnaissance Division

Her mission is to find a hero who doesn't want to be found, but this Colby Agency P.I. always gets her man. She just doesn't count on the danger surrounding her target...or her irresistible attraction to him.

#1158 HIS BEST FRIEND'S BABY by Mallory Kane
Black Hills Brotherhood

When his best friend's baby is kidnapped, the rugged survival expert is on call to help rescue her child. As they follow the kidnapper's trail up a remote mountain, they must battle the elements and an undeniable passion.

#1159 PEEK-A-BOO PROTECTOR by Rita Herron
Seeing Double

The sheriff admires the work of the child advocate, but her latest charge, an abandoned baby, is the target of merciless kidnappers. Her life is on the line, and he's discovering that protecting her may be more than just a job....

#1160 COVERT COOTCHIE-COOTCHIE-COO
by Ann Voss Peterson
Seeing Double

Someone wants to harm the baby boy left aboard his ship, and the captain hires a tenacious P.I. to get some answers. As they work together to keep the child safe, startling truths are not the only things they uncover....